P9-DEV-016

The
Other Side
of the
Fence

ALSO BY JEAN URE:

You Win Some, You Lose Some
After Thursday

The
Other Side
of the
Fence

Jean Ure

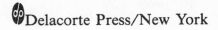Delacorte Press/New York

Published by
Delacorte Press
The Bantam Doubleday Dell Publishing Group, Inc.
1 Dag Hammarskjold Plaza
New York, New York 10017

This work was first published in Great Britain
by The Bodley Head Ltd.

Manufactured in the United States of America

First U.S.A. printing

Library of Congress Cataloging in Publication Data

Ure, Jean.
The other side of the fence/by Jean Ure.
p. cm.
Summary: The timid son of a wealthy businessman and an abused
sixteen-year-old girl lacking self-esteem flee from their respective
homes, accidentally meet, and work out their problems while rooming
together in a condemned building in London.
ISBN 0-385-29627-4
[1. Self-confidence—Fiction. 2. Self-respect—Fiction.
3. England—Fiction.] I. Title.
PZ7.U640t 1988
[Fic]—dc19   87-27184
CIP
AC

1
Chapter

It was early in the morning when Richard awoke. He found himself slumped sideways in the driver's seat with his head resting against the window, his legs uncomfortably wedged beneath the dashboard. Slowly and cautiously he coaxed his protesting limbs into movement. He had obviously been sleeping with one of his hands trapped underneath him, for it hung now like a lead weight at his side, limp and useless. His right leg was crippled with cramp and his neck seemed to be stuck permanently at an angle of forty-five degrees. A VW was no place for spending the night; not when you were six feet tall.

He sat for a moment or two, massaging his various aches and pains, trying to collect his scattered senses and work out where he was. Through the window he could see, only dimly without his glasses, rain-washed fields that stretched bare and sodden into the far, flat distance. Ahead of him lay a road, empty and unfamiliar, winding through the bleak March countryside like a roll of black ribbon.

He remembered.

What the devil do you think this place is? Freedom Hall? This is your mother's home, and I will not have it polluted! If you choose to conduct yourself like some diseased creature that's crawled out of a sewer then that's up to you, but by God I won't have it brought back here! You can get out right now—and as far as I'm concerned you can stay out!

At ten o'clock at night there'd only been one place he could think of to go, and that was up to the Lakes, to Sue and Dermot. The flat wasn't any good. At Jan's suggestion, in the interest of economy, they had given it up for the vacation. Their landlady had rented it for six weeks to someone from abroad. In any case, he didn't know, now, whether he would be going back there or not.

He peered at his watch and saw that it was almost seven o'clock. It had been past midnight when he turned off the highway. It had suddenly struck him, just a few miles short of Crewe: there wasn't any point in going up north to the Lake District. Sue and Dermot wouldn't be there. They were in Switzerland, enjoying the snow. His mother, blushing a little and a bit flustered because it was in front of his father, had told them about it.

"Sue and Dermot have gone to Switzerland. . . . Have you ever been to Switzerland, Jan?"

Jan had said no, never.

"Oh, but you ought to! You really must. It's quite beautiful, all the snow, and the blue sky, and the mountains. Just like the postcards."

His mother had seemed really happy, laughing and talking, not nearly as nervous as she usually was. It was Jan's presence that had made her relax. She had liked Jan; they had gotten along well together. That was the irony of it: they had all gotten along with Jan.

"I'm so glad you're making nice friends," his mother had said, out in the kitchen on that first night before they went to bed. His father had agreed.

"Thank the Lord you haven't got into the long-haired, drug-taking set."

Kate had stuck up a thumb and said, "Not half bad!" which for Kate was praise indeed. Notoriously hard to please, was Kate. She'd almost never approved of anyone he brought home—not that he'd brought that many people. He'd always been a bit of a loner, a bit of an outsider. He'd never really met anyone he could relax and be at ease with until he went to college and met Jan.

He pressed the tips of his fingers to his eyeballs for a moment. His eyes felt hot and aching, as they had last night after the showdown with his father. Before the showdown it had all been going so well. They had spent the afternoon playing bridge, Richard partnering his mother (to keep her from being bullied) and his father partnering Jan. His father and Jan had won all three rubbers. Mr. Islip had been delighted. He had said that Jan had more card sense than Richard and his mother put together.

So extremely pleased had he been that as Jan was leaving he had proffered his hand and said, "I shall be happy to see you here again. Any time. You're most welcome." Behind his back, out of vision, Kate had made elaborate swooning motions. Richard's mother had beamed and nodded, pleased because her husband was pleased, because everyone was happy. Little had she known how soon that happiness was to be shattered.

He and Jan had driven to the station in time for Jan to catch the eight thirty train.

"Don't forget," Jan had said, "what we agreed: as soon as you get back, you're going to tell them. Right?"

He should never have allowed himself to be talked into it. He had known all along it would be disastrous.

He reached into the glove compartment, feeling for his glasses. His mother had been weeping when he left the house. He wasn't sure whether she was weeping because of what he had revealed or because, for the first time ever, he had stood up to his father, had taken him at his word. His father had told him he could get out—which in itself was nothing new, since Mr. Islip was in the habit of telling his offspring they could get out. What was new was that Richard had done so. He had snatched up the car keys and left. His mother had come running out after him down the drive, her face awash in a sea of tears.

"Richard, don't—he didn't mean it! You mustn't, you'll have an accident, you're in no fit state . . . Richard, please! Come back!"

He hated seeing his mother upset. He hated even more to be the one who was upsetting her, but the influence of Jan had still been strong upon him; his father had said things that were not to be lived with.

8

He knew that they had been said in the heat of the moment, but he also knew that in his innermost self they were what his father held true. And so he had left, and there could be no going back.

He settled his glasses on his nose, pushing them up with the tip of his left index finger. The world outside the car became clearer, and more dismal. He could see that it was raining, that the morning sky was leaden and overcast. His mind felt no less so. He leaned forward and switched on the ignition. The gas gauge registered almost empty. He had his checkbook in his pocket, a credit card in his wallet; he could drive to the nearest service station and fill up the tank . . . and then what? Then where would he go? Then what would he do?

Sue and Dermot were away, Jan by now would be making tracks for the Cotswolds and a vacation job with disabled kids. Aunts, uncles, grandparents, all were out of the question. Sooner seek refuge in the local doss house—if there still were such places. He had read about doss houses in George Orwell, a book that Jan had pressed upon him: *Down and Out in Paris and London*. Jan had said it would do him good to learn how the other half lived, and so, obediently, he had read it.

"Not quite such fun, is it," Jan had said, "when you're on the other side of the fence?"

He had had to agree that it wasn't, because of course such poverty as Orwell described was quite appalling; but that was way back before the war. Things had changed since then—or had they? Suddenly he wasn't quite so sure. What did one do when one had no job, no money (or at any rate, precious little), and no home to go back to?

He sat at the wheel of the car, waiting for panic to set in. It didn't. Instead there came a curious sense of well-being, almost of exhilaration. For the first time in all his eighteen years he was on his own. No one to shout at him, no one to shove him around, no one to tell him that he was feeble and spineless and ought to be doing something other than that which he wanted to do. The decisions, now, were up to him.

With sudden determination he let out the clutch. Step number one, he would find a service station; step number two, he would fill up the tank. When he had done both of those things he would decide what to do next.

2
Chapter

Bonny stood by the side of the road, a forlorn wisp of a figure in the early morning murk. The hem of her skirt was caked with mud, clinging cold and clammy about her legs; her feet, in thin suede boots that had never been intended for tramping the winter countryside, were frozen almost solid. When she tried wiggling her toes it felt as if each separate one were encased in a thimble of ice.

It was a bad time of the year for hitchhiking. A bad time of the year, a bad time of the week. Seven o'clock on a Sunday morning? *You must be joking!* She could hear Jake saying it, his voice full of impatience and scorn. Probably if she had any sense she'd have waited till payday and gone down by train, but payday wasn't till the end of the month; she couldn't possibly have held out until then. When Bonny did things, she had to do them immediately. Acting without thinking, was what Jake called it. So, all right, perhaps she *had* acted without thinking, just packing her bag and running out of the house at six o'clock on a dark March morning, but if she had, it was his fault. He had run out before she had.

Her fingers in her coat pocket closed over the note that he had left. It had been there yesterday evening, pushed under her bedroom door, waiting for her when she got back from a day spent behind the checkout at Matheson's: *Bonny, Have gone to Ireland. Have fun. Jake.*

That was all; no indication of when, if ever, he intended to come back. He had been threatening it for ages—"I've got to get the hell out of this dump, it's stifling me!" He had said it so often, she had thought it was just one of those things. One of those things that people said and never did, like Donovan saying he was going to find himself a steady job, and Julie always going on about putting bombs under people. Julie wouldn't ever really put a bomb under anyone, any more than Donovan was likely ever to find himself a steady job. Or Jake get the hell out—except that Jake had.

She blinked as tears mingled with the drizzling rain and blurred her view. Had the others known what he intended? On that last night, sitting there at the kitchen table, eating hamburgers and French fries that Bonny had provided, had they known then? Both of them sitting there, knowing, looking at Bonny not knowing. Feeling sorry for her. Feeling contemptuous.

12

"Dumb idiot!" That would be Julie. Julie was like Jake: *she* wouldn't feel any sympathy. Donovan might. "Hey, now, man, you can't do that to the chick!" But he had done it. Because he was a louse.

Jake Armitage was a *louse*.

Angrily, Bonny bunched up a fist and scrunched away the tears. So what? If Jake didn't want her, she would go to people who did. The only people who ever had. Nobby and Bo; *they* wanted her. They had told her, when she had left the shelter of their cottage in Southampton and gone running off up to Crewe to be with Jake, they had told her then, "This will always be your home. No matter where you go or what you do, we shall always be here." When Nobby and Bo said something, they meant it. It wasn't just empty words, as it was with other people.

Jake had said that she was stupid and naive.

"Just a couple of old dykes, aren't they? Couple of old dykes who took a shine to you. Go back tomorrow, you'll find they've adopted someone else."

She hated him for saying that. Jake always ruined everything with his sneering and his jeering.

Jake was a *louse*.

From the bare brown fields opposite, an icy wind was cutting. Bonny sneezed and huddled further into the depths of her coat. If she got a cold it would be all Jake's fault. Thirty minutes she had been waiting here, in the drizzling rain on the damp grass shoulder. Only a dozen cars had she counted, and all but two of them going the wrong way. She sneezed again and groped in vain in the depths of her canvas bag for a dry handkerchief. All she could find was a bunch of sodden tissues.

A Rolls-Royce had topped the crest of the road. It

13

bowled majestically forward and glided straight past, without so much as a glance in Bonny's direction. It was only what she had expected. One didn't get lifts from people in Rolls-Royces. Come to that, one didn't get them from people in Mercedes or Jaguars. *Or* people in BMWs.

Or people in Volvos.

Jake loathed people who drove big cars. But then, Jake loathed so many things.

The road was empty again; not a vehicle in sight. Bonny sighed and curled up her toes inside her boots. She wondered what Donovan and Julie were going to think when they crawled out of bed at about lunchtime and discovered she wasn't there. Nothing very much, in all probability. Probably wouldn't even notice. They might just notice on Monday, but even that wasn't a foregone conclusion. On account of not working, they never got out of bed until about midday. Bonny had been the only one in that setup to have regular employment. Julie didn't believe in it, and Donovan was all mouth. Never had a proper job in his life. Jake, just occasionally, had given a hand moving scenery at the local rep, but not very often. Jake didn't approve of the rep. "A tool of the establishment" was what he called it. He went there only when really pushed, or when there was an actress he happened to like. That snooty Elaine cow had really turned him on. Not that he'd got anywhere with her; she was far too grand for the likes of him—though that hadn't stopped her coming round to Factory Lane night after night after the show and sitting there jawing till the small hours. It was all right for the rest of them; they didn't have to be up the next morning. Just lay there snoring, like a load of pigs,

14

while Bonny stumbled around with her eyes gummed together trying not to trip over them.

She bet it would be Wednesday or Thursday before anyone actually cottoned on to the fact that she wasn't there anymore. Miss Amphlett, at Matheson's, would probably miss her before they did. Miss Amphlett would be furious.

"Where is Miss McEvoy?" she would demand of one of the others; Jackie or Sandra or Mrs. Dunbarton. They would shake their heads and say they didn't know. "Late again! This is the third time this month."

Miss Amphlett would take out her notebook and the silver pen that she kept hanging around her neck on a chain, and she would write down Bonny's name and put a big black star against it. Bonny was always having big black stars put by her name; more than five meant you were liable to be given your marching orders. She probably had about ten by now, so one more wasn't going to make much difference. Miss Amphlett could put as many as she liked. By lunchtime she would really be frothing. She would spend the rest of the day bawling people out and putting big black stars as fast as she could. She would never discover where Bonny had gone.

Nobby and Bo wouldn't like that; they would say it was letting people down. Bonny scowled and humped her canvas bag more securely over her shoulder. So what? Miss Amphlett was only a capitalist lackey anyway. Jake had said so. Jake had said—

Jake had said, Jake had said—she didn't *care* anymore what Jake had said. Jake was a pig, and she was going to forget him.

The rain was falling faster now, more of a downpour

15

than a drizzle. She was going to get very wet. A sudden belt of it came slashing into her face, almost throwing her off balance. Her beret—the little red beret with the pom-pom, which Bo had knitted for her—went flying from her head. She snatched it up just in time, before it could be whirled away across the road and into the fields beyond, but already it was sodden, like the hem of her skirt. Like her boots, and her feet inside them.

Misery engulfed her. She was cold and she was wet and she hadn't any money. She wanted to be back home, in Southampton, with Nobby and Bo and the cats. How much longer was she going to have to stand here?

A flash of chrome caught her eye: a big, powder blue Mercedes had appeared on the horizon. She pulled out her ball of sodden tissues. It was no use crying. Crying was not going to get her to Southampton. Men hated tears. Jake always said that sniveling females drove him mad.

The Mercedes was approaching fast. Bonny gave her eyes one final scrub and determinedly stepped forward. Mercedes or not, this time they were going to *stop*.

3
Chapter

Richard turned up the collar of his old leather jacket and trudged onward through the gloom. In one hand he was carrying the spare gas can from the trunk of the VW: it was empty. So was the gas tank. The car had given up the ghost about a mile back. It was entirely his own fault, just as everything always was.

What the devil is the point of carrying a spare gas can if you don't intend to keep it filled with gas? Useless. Spineless. Sloppy-minded. Inefficient. He wondered what it must be like to be perfect.

Around a bend in the road he came upon a large sign that said SERVICE STATION 400 YARDS ON LEFT. LAST BEFORE HIGHWAY. That was a relief. The highway must be the M-6, which he had turned off last night. He could either carry on northward up to Crewe or back down south to . . . to where? And for what?

He would decide that when he was mobile again. First things first: until he had a full tank of gas he wasn't going anywhere.

A few yards further on he passed a girl standing by the roadside in a long flouncing skirt down to her ankles and a baggy tweed coat that looked like a man's. She was trying to attract the attention of a big, powder blue Mercedes that had just appeared over the brow of the hill. The Mercedes flashed past in a disdainful dazzle of chrome plate, without so much as a backward glance: the girl at once turned and sent a furious one-fingered gesture winging after it. Richard thought, but could not be certain, that she also added an invitation to the driver to "Go screw himself." He smiled grimly. Exactly the sort of female to give his old man an apoplexy.

The girl obviously felt his gaze upon her, for she swiveled around suspiciously to confront him. The coat *was* a man's. The buttons were on the wrong side and the pockets hung down almost to her knees. It was the sort of garment Kate sometimes came home with, all proud and happy, from the local thrift shop, only to be told nervously by their mother, "Don't let your father see you in that."

This girl looked to be about the same age as Kate, maybe a bit younger. She stared at him haughtily as he passed, for all the world as if it was he rather than she who had just made the obscene gesture. Richard swung his empty gas can. He wondered what she was doing, hitching lifts all by herself in that crazy getup at seven fifteen on a Sunday morning. She was hardly dressed for the occasion.

He threw a last backward glance over his shoulder; the girl tilted her chin at him. He noticed that the chestnut curls escaping from beneath the woolly red beret she wore slanted on her head were plastered flat with the rain. The beret itself was sodden and limp. At this rate she was going to get thoroughly wet before she even started.

He squelched on his way through the roadside mire. Could it be that there were others in the world as futile and incompetent as he? It would certainly be a comfort to feel that one was not alone.

Bonny stood watching him go. She tossed her head contemptuously. Stuck-up idiot! Who did he think he was, looking at her like that? Queen of England? He could think himself lucky she hadn't been swearing at *him*. She would have, for two cents. Jake always said her language was foul, though Jake was hardly in any position to talk. His was fouler than absolutely anyone's.

She clamped a hand to her head as a sudden squall of rain almost removed her beret for the second time. Trickles of water ran down into her eyes, quivering and dripping at the end of her nose like the horrible dewdrops that had quivered and dripped from the nose of Miss Amphlett in cold weather. She was glad she wasn't ever going to have to see Miss Amphlett again. She didn't care if it *was* letting people down, she couldn't possibly have stayed on for another whole week—not without Jake to go back to. Surely Nobby and Bo would see that.

From out of her canvas bag she pulled an old sweater and draped it over her head, knotting the sleeves together beneath her chin. It probably looked stupid, but what did she care? Jake wasn't there to see, and there wasn't anyone else who mattered. Certainly not those youths who frowned at her for only saying screw. She could have said far worse words than that if she'd felt so inclined. Prig.

Richard had reached the service station. He had filled up the spare can with gas and had paid for it with money out of his pocket, which left him with precisely £2.25 to face the world. He still had his checkbook and his credit card, but the credit card only guaranteed him up to a limited amount, and he wasn't sure how many times he would be able to get away with using it before someone found out and put a stop to it. He was already overdrawn by forty-eight pounds. He had been hoping to clear up the debt before next term by putting in a few weeks working for the old man, but that was obviously out of the question now.

He went into the men's room to wash up, but there wasn't any warm water and the paper towel dispenser was empty. He felt crumpled and unclean; hungry, as well. Back home in Cheltenham they would soon be sitting down to a breakfast of cereal, toast and marmalade, sausage, bacon, and eggs. He glanced at his watch: nearly quarter to eight. Perhaps he ought just to give his mother a quick call and reassure her that he was still in the land of the living. Set her mind at rest; stop her having nightmares about highway pileups and head-on collisions. If his old man answered he would simply say, polite but cold, "This is Richard. May I speak to Mother please?"

There was a telephone in the garage parking lot. Just for a moment as he punched out the number he had doubts, but then the receiver was lifted at the other end and it was Kate. He wasn't sure what Kate's reaction to his revelations was likely to be—she had been out when he got back from dropping Jan off at the station and so had missed all the fun—but he had always firmly believed his younger sister to be unshockable. He didn't *think* she would be perturbed—assuming, that is, she had been told the truth—but of course one could never be certain.

"Kate?" he said. He said it hesitantly, testing the water, just in case. He didn't think he could bear it if Kate were to hang up on him.

"Richard?" Her voice came shrieking excitedly, high and shrill, into his ear. There was a slight note of accusation in it, but no trace, so far as he could judge, of hostility.

"Yes," he said, relieved.

"Where *are* you?"

"In a service station near the M-Six. Is M—"

"Service station near the M-Six? What are you doing near the M-Six?" And then, before he could answer— *"Didn't* you put the cat among the pigeons. Honestly!"

She sounded almost as if she were congratulating him for it—almost as if she *admired* him. Imagine that! The poor old worm turning at last.

"I'd never have guessed," she said. "At least, I s'pose I *might* have done, if—"

If what? At that moment another voice came on the line.

21

"Richard? What do you want?"

He licked his lips. Polite but cold. "I should like to speak to my mother please."

"Your mother has no wish to speak to you. I should have thought after last night you would know better than to suggest it. What are you trying to do? Make her even more ill than you've already done?"

He wanted to shout, "*I* didn't make her ill, it's you that does that! You, with your blustering and your bullyboy tactics!" He wanted to, but he didn't, because the words wouldn't come. They would have come for Kate, they would have come for Sue, but it wasn't Richard's way.

"I just wanted to let her know," he said, "that I'm all right."

"Oh! So you call it being all right, do you? You call it being all right to—"

"That I'm safe," said Richard. "That I haven't had a crash or anything. I just wanted her to know."

"And what makes you think that she would care to know? What makes you think that she has the slightest interest anymore in *what* you choose to do? Go out and kill yourself! Go out and—"

Sickened, he put down the receiver. He had done what he could; at least his mother would be able to relax in the knowledge that he was still alive and not lying decapitated somewhere on the highway. Kate would pass the message on even if the old man didn't.

He thought about his mother as he left the service station. He didn't believe that bit about her not wanting to speak to him. She might have been upset just at first—probably any mother would be—but he didn't

22

feel that she'd been devastated. After all, it was hardly the end of the world. And she had *liked* Jan.

He must send Jan a postcard. Explain what had happened. Say that it had been disastrous.

No, he wouldn't say that. Jan might think he was hurling accusations—"It was your fault, you were the one that told me to do it!" It wasn't anyone's fault but his. He should have trusted his instincts and kept quiet, even if it did mean living a lie. Lies, sometimes, were safer than the truth. He only wished to God—

No, he didn't. Wishing was a sign of weakness. From now on he must learn to be strong and decisive, like Kate. The first place he came to he would stop and have breakfast, and he would buy a postcard and a stamp. That would be his immediate objective. When he had done that he would think what to do next.

The girl in the red beret was still standing by the side of the road. She had wrapped her head up in a sweater. She was obviously having no luck with the hitchhiking. As he came toward her a Ford Granada went rocketing past at eighty miles an hour, followed in quick succession by a gaudy pink Cadillac and a family sedan full of children and dogs. A trailer truck looked more likely prey, but the driver only winked at her from the cab and went on without stopping. The thin shoulders drooped dispiritedly. She seemed to have lost all heart for even a token gesture of defiance.

Richard paused and shifted his can of gas from one hand to the other. He wasn't as a rule a great one for striking up conversations with strangers—introverted, Jan said he was; Kate more kindly said he was shy—but today was different. Today was the start of a new era.

"Hi," he said, and he attempted a grin: casual, careless, the way Jan was. "You don't seem to be having much luck."

The girl turned at once to stare at him. She regarded him balefully from out of the folds of her sweater.

"It's a bad road."

"Ah."

There was a pause. Richard stood awkwardly, wanting to say something more but not quite knowing what. The girl stood waiting. She reminded him in an odd sort of way of Jan. She was small and compact, with the same cropped curly hair and determined chin. The only difference—well, not the *only* difference, obviously—was that her cheeks were covered in freckles and she had this tiny round blob of a nose, at present mistrustfully wrinkled.

"I suppose"—he waved a hand vaguely in the direction of the sky—"the weather doesn't exactly help."

She shrugged, as if dismissing both the weather and himself as of no account.

"Probably not. Excuse me."

A car was approaching; an old Rover, upright and stately, of the kind his father had once owned. The girl sidestepped and began thumbing vigorously. To no avail: the Rover sailed serenely on. It was exactly what his old man would have done had he been driving.

Richard cleared his throat. "Which way are you headed?"

There was a moment of silence, then, "South," said Bonny. It was the snob who had disapproved of her language. Not much chance him giving her a lift. Still, anything was worth a try. She tightened the sleeves of her sweater under her chin. "Which way are you?"

"I can go south," said Richard. He could go any which way. It was immaterial to him. Just so long as he bought that postcard. "You want a ride?" That was good, that was what Jan would have said. He began to feel more confident. "I'm afraid it'll mean a bit of a trek, just to begin with. I ran out of gas. The car's about half a mile back."

"Okay."

She didn't mind walking half a mile, provided it meant she was going to get somewhere at the end of it. They set off together, Richard walking on the road, Bonny squidging along at his side on the grass shoulder. He didn't ask her why she was wearing a sweater wrapped round her head—just as well, or she'd have given him short shrift; after all, it must be pretty obvious—but he did ask if he could relieve her of her canvas bag. Bonny shook her head and clung to it protectively. She wasn't falling for that one. Only let him get his hands on something of value and he'd be off like greased lightning.

"Well, if you're sure," said Richard.

She was sure; she wasn't born yesterday. Just because he spoke with a posh accent didn't mean a thing. These pinch-nosed types were often the worst. Con their grandmothers out of their last pair of drawers, that was what Jake said.

They reached the car, a little black VW decorated in swirling loops of gold and silver. It was pointing in the wrong direction for going south.

"I'll just fill her up," said Richard.

Bonny watched as he unscrewed the cap on the gas can. He could only have about two gallons in there.

25

Two gallons wasn't going to get them very far, even in a mini.

"When you say south," she said, "how far south do you mean?"

Richard tipped up the can. "As far south as you like." He could go to Land's End if that was what she wanted. At least it would be something positive. "How far did you have in mind?"

Bonny looked at him suspiciously. She hoped that wasn't intended as a smart remark.

"I'm going to Southampton," she said.

"Southampton's all right by me." He had never been to Southampton. He tossed the empty gas can into the trunk and walked around to the driver's door. "Do you want to jump in?"

Bonny hesitated. Never accept lifts from strange men, that was what they were always drumming into you, wasn't it? And here was she, about to step into some showy little souped-up VW driven by a chinless wonder who didn't seem to care whether he went north, south, or all points in between, just so long as he had someone to go there with.

"All right?"

He had leaned across and opened the passenger door. Bonny threw a quick, cautious glance inside the car. If there was an old dirty raincoat or a pair of kid gloves stashed away under the dashboard she would be off up the road before you could say knife.

There wasn't. All she could see was a handbook and something by George Orwell: *Down and Out in . . .* she couldn't decipher the rest. Not even a *Penthouse* or a *Playboy* ; just the handbook and George Orwell. George Orwell was all right, Jake had said so. Bourgeois, of course, but he had written some fairly okay stuff. Perhaps she had misjudged the chinless wonder after all. Now that she came to study him more closely she could see that he wasn't as old as she'd first thought, probably not even as old as Jake. It was the glasses that made him seem so. In fact, when you discounted the glasses, he had quite a reasonable sort of face, and furthermore he had fair hair. She always felt that you could trust men with fair hair. Jake's had been black as soot and thick as a dish mop. She supposed, really, that she had never *completely* trusted Jake.

"We'll just stop off somewhere," said Richard, "and get the tank filled up; then we'll be on our way." He pushed his glasses back up his nose. "Okay?"

Bonny took a breath: "Okay."

One had, after all, to take *some* chances in life. And if worst came to worst . . .

But maybe it wouldn't. Maybe, at last, her luck was changing.

4
Chapter

"Nice car," said Bonny. She indicated the whirling hoops of gold and silver that adorned the VW's hood. "Great paint job."

"Yes." Jan had been responsible for that. His old man, of course, had looked at it askance, but fortunately it wasn't anything to do with the old man.

"I like cars that've been painted up." Jake, for a short time, had had an old Ford Mustang, all reds and oranges and luminous shades of purple. Bonny had begged and begged him to teach her how to drive, but he never would. He had said she was too stupid to be trusted. Jake was always saying she was stupid. Jake really was such a *louse*.

Bonny kicked off her sodden boots and put her feet up on the dashboard.

"You a student," she said, "or what?"

"Student."

"At college?" She didn't know why she bothered to ask: you could tell, just by looking at him, that he would be at university. "We ought to introduce ourselves." She wriggled her toes in the red woolly socks, which had been knitted by Bo to go with the beret. ("Her Little Red Riding Hood outfit," Jake had called it when he had first seen it.) "I'm Bonny McEvoy. Who're you?"

"Richard," he said. "Richard Islip."

Richard. She studied him critically for a moment as he drove, trying to assess whether or not he looked like a Richard. "What do people call you? Do they call you Rick or something?"

"Mostly they just call me Richard." He said it almost apologetically, as if it were his fault that he was mostly just Richard. "What about you? Why are you c-called Bonny? Is it a nickname?"

"No." She sat up, proudly. "It's my real name, on my birth certificate. They thought I looked bonny, and so that's what they called me. It was either that or Hedwig."

"*Head* Wig?"

Bonny nodded happily. She enjoyed telling people the story of how she had come by her name. "The lady who found me was called Hedwig; she was a cleaning person in this hospital, and she found this bundle wrapped up in a shoe box with a note pinned on to it saying 'Please take care of my baby, I can't look after her,' and nobody knew who I was or where I came from and so they called me Bonny. Imagine if it had been *Hed*wig."

29

When she told Jake he had said, "Yeah. Imagine if any of it had been true," which wasn't fair, because some of it *was* true. Quite a lot, as a matter of fact.

All Richard said was, "I once knew someone named Thackeray."

She wasn't interested in someone named Thackeray.

"Thackeray Jones. That's pretty awful."

Thackeray Jones, Thackeray Smith, or Thackeray anything else. This was *her* story, about *her*.

"What happened," she said, "they showed my picture on the television, in this shoe box, all wrapped up, and my mother saw it and she came to the hospital and said who she was and took me away again." Just for a little while. It wasn't long before she found another man to run off with and Bonny was dumped again. Still, she'd had a few months of proper homelife. Not that she could actually remember any of it.

"My father" she said, and paused for effect, ". . . was a pop star."

"Really?"

"Yes. He was American. He was over here from the States doing this tour. That's when my mother met him, at this nightclub where she was a hostess."

Jake at this point had broken up. He had given a great hoot of laughter and said, "Hostess! No wonder she got herself knocked up!" Bonny still couldn't understand what was so funny about it. She had chosen *hostess* because it sounded classy. She waited to see if Richard would laugh, but he didn't. Instead, very seriously, he said, "G-gosh!" ("Gosh! Cwikey! Cwackerjack!" She could just hear Jake mimicking him.) "How romantic!"

"Yes. It was." So sucks to you, Jake Armitage.

30

"They were ever so much in love. Unfortunately . . ." She stared out of the window at the rain-drenched countryside. "He went and got killed in this airplane crash before I was born, so I never knew him. I s'pose you weren't thinking of stopping anywhere, were you? I'm absolutely starving."

Yes, so was he; it had temporarily slipped his mind. He had been going to pull in somewhere and have breakfast—and buy that postcard for Jan.

He managed to buy the postcard (the stamp would have to wait for later) and settled down to write it over a breakfast of soggy toast and strange, metallic-tasting coffee. He found it difficult, thinking what to say. People like Jan, like Kate, who positively enjoyed taking on the rest of the world, had no idea what they were asking when they demanded of people like him that they, too, should stand up and be counted: this is me, this is how I am, take it or leave it. It wasn't that easy.

He looked again at the blank postcard.

"I always have that trouble," said Bonny. "Why don't you just put, 'X marks the spot,' or, 'Having a wonderful time wish you were here?' That's what I do."

He made a face. "It's not that sort of a card."

What he needed was something that would alert without causing alarm. He didn't want to give the impression that he was backing down. He wasn't backing down. He wasn't ratting, he wasn't running out; but he had to have a breathing space. Jan would surely understand.

He contented himself in the end with three simple sentences: *Reception not too good. Am staying away for a bit. Will be in touch.* Only after some hesitation,

31

aware that Bonny, with quite open and unabashed interest, was watching as he wrote, did he add, *Love from R.* He wasn't exactly proud of it, but it was the best he could manage.

They got back into the car and drove on, down the thruway, Bonny chattering practically nonstop.

". . . And then when I was about *two* . . . And then when I got to *school* age . . . and then when I was four*teen* . . ."

He had thought Kate was a talker, but she had nothing on Bonny. He listened in a kind of bemused fascination as the details unrolled.

". . . Then after *that* they started trying to foster me, sent me out to all these places. Only they had to stop after a bit 'cause people said I was unmanageable. I had these temper tantrums when I used to go mad and throw things. Once I threw an iron at someone and knocked her out. She deserved to get knocked out. She was horrible. She used to make me eat bread and margarine and lock me in a cupboard.

Richard turned, appalled, to look at her. "She didn't."

"She did," said Bonny. "She was really horrible. Anyway, after I bashed her they took me away and sent me to this other place. Some woman named Foskett. She was absolutely bananas."

The bananas woman had made her read the Bible every day.

"I mean, *every day* . . . that's bonkers, isn't it? It's potty. I couldn't stand it. I tore the pages out and stuffed them down the toilet. The toilet got blocked up. They said they weren't going to send me anywhere else after that, they said people couldn't cope with me.

They said I didn't deserve to be fostered. I told them,"
said Bonny, "I didn't *want* to be."

But then, willy-nilly, she had been sent to this couple in Southampton with the unlikely names of Nobby
and Bo. Nobby had been someone's secretary and Bo
had been a nurse, and they were both quite old, at least
sixty, but they had three cats called Simeon, Barnaby,
and Esmeralda, and they did jigsaw puzzles and cross-
words, and far from being unable to cope they had
actually told Bonny that "there would always be a
home there for me, *always*." She said it with such fer-
vent conviction it was impossible not to believe her. He
may have had his doubts about the bread-and-marga-
rine woman and the bananas lady, but he couldn't have
any doubts about Nobby and Bo.

He wondered if Bonny habitually poured out the
most intimate details of her life history to every Tom,
Dick, or Harry who crossed her path. It embarrassed
him, hearing some of the things she related, but at the
same time he couldn't help being just a little bit flat-
tered. No one had ever confided in him before. They
confided in Jan because Jan was outgoing, but he was
too stiff and awkward to invite personal confessions.
He had once gone out with the sister of a school friend
and she had written him a note the next day saying she
didn't want to go out with him again because "You're
all full of tensions and make me feel uncomfortable." It
didn't seem that he made Bonny feel uncomfortable.
Maybe she hadn't noticed him being all full of tensions. Maybe to her he seemed quite normal and re-
laxed.

He was just starting to feel good about it when she
said, "You don't *talk* very much, do you?"

33

The way she said it, she definitely made it sound as if not talking very much was abnormal.

"Where d'you come from?" She looked at him accusingly. "Up north?"

He heard himself apologizing. "Cheltenham, actually."

Chelt'nem, ecktewllay. Bonny gave a little wriggle on her seat.

"Is *Chelt*'nem where you're at college?"

"No, it's—where my parents live."

"Ah." She thought it over a bit, then, "What d'you do at college?" she asked.

"I'm majoring in history."

"Hist'ry?" She brightened. He had obviously said something right for once. "*I* like hist'ry. It was my best subject. I'm just reading about the Fire of London. Have you done the Fire of London?"

He shook his head; apologizing again.

"It's a bit outside my period."

"Why? What's your period?"

"Well . . . medieval, mainly."

"That's Crusades and things."

"Yes."

"And the Plague. I've just read about the Plague. It's in this book, *Forever Amber*. Have you read it? You ought, if you're doing hist'ry. It's all about this woman that's a whore—well, not exactly a *whore* . . ."

He listened gravely while she told him the story of *Forever Amber*.

". . . And then they get the plague and the buboes burst and there's all this black gunge, and everything stinking . . . You ought to get it out the library. It'll tell you a thing or two. Not that it's medieval, but it's

34

all hist'ry." She lapsed for a few rare moments into silence, then, "What d'you actually do with it?" she said. "Medieval hist'ry? I mean . . . when you've got it? What d'you do with it?"

It was a question he had often puzzled over himself. When he had got it (assuming that he did get it, which now was by no means certain) what did he do with it? He was as undecided about that as about everything else.

"It doesn't really seem as if it'd be much use," said Bonny, "does it?"

"What do *you* do?" said Richard.

"Me?" Bonny put a finger into her mouth and tore off a flap of skin. "I'm an actress. I've been acting with the rep theater up in Crewe."

"Really?" That was interesting; he liked the theater. "What plays have you done?"

"Oh . . . this and that." The last one she could remember, when Jake had moved scenery and Elaine had still been around, was *The Merchant of Venice*. "*The Merchant of Venice,*" she said.

"We did that at school! I was Bassanio. What part did you play?"

Elaine had played Portia, standing in the middle of the stage in a black robe and a flat hat stuck on her head, spouting about the quality of mercy. Everyone had said how fantastic she was.

"I played Portia," said Bonny.

Richard turned to look at her. He seemed surprised. "I'd have said you were more like a Nerissa."

What was he going on about, more like an Irissa? Who was Irissa? Some Irish character?

"Did you go and train at a drama school?"

"Yes," said Bonny. "I went to the Royal Academy of Dramatic Art."

"RADA? A boy I was at school with went to RADA! His name's Philip Russell. Did you ever meet him?"

"I may have done. I can't remember. There were too many people." Bonny leaned forward to squint at the road. "I think this might be the turnoff," she said.

It was growing late in the evening when they finally reached the outskirts of Southampton. Bonny said that when they got to the old ladies' she would ask if Richard could stay the night.

"If you haven't got anywhere else to go, that is."

He hadn't got anywhere else to go. The realization suddenly hit him: What was he *doing,* driving aimlessly around the countryside?

Taking Bonny to Southampton, that was what he was doing. And after he had taken her?

Tomorrow morning?

What?

He swallowed, making an effort to speak normally. "Are you quite sure they won't mind?"

"They won't mind," said Bonny. "They never mind anything I do. They're that sort of people."

She seemed very certain. He wondered if she had ever actually put it to the test.

They were nearing the end of their journey. Bonny, who had spent the last few miles curled into the depths of her seat like a dormouse, her arms wrapped around her legs, her knees hunched up to her chin, now sat up straight, wide awake and watchful, staring out at the road ahead with its long line of lights winking and blinking into the far distance.

"Which way?" said Richard.

"Turn right by the side of the big hotel—Highfield Way. Just opposite the square."

Highfield Way was dark and leafy, tree-lined on one side with large Victorian houses set back from the road; on the other was the square. Near the end it petered out into a lane, with a pair of old red-brick semidetached cottages, outside which Bonny directed him to stop.

"I'll just go and tell them we're here," she said. "Then you can come in."

He watched from the driver's seat as she ran confidently up the path to the first of the cottages. He couldn't help wondering what his old man would say if he were to try turning up in the middle of the night with a stranger in tow.

What the devil do you think this place is? Freedom Hall?

Suddenly, as he sat waiting, Bonny turned and gestured at him. She seemed agitated. He rolled down the window and stuck his head out. "What's the matter?"

"Nobody's answering!"

"Try again."

"I have tried! I've tried and tried. *I don't think anybody's here.*"

5
Chapter

He left the car and walked across the road to join her. At close quarters, he couldn't help noticing, the place looked almost derelict.

"You try," said Bonny.

Obediently he lifted the old brass horseshoe knocker and let it fall.

"Not like that!" Bonny snatched at it, impatient. "Like this!"

The noise of the knocker as wielded by Bonny went crashing and reverberating into the night. The reverberations died away, to be succeeded by silence.

"They've got to be out," said Richard. He pushed open the flap of the letter box and stooped to call through it. "Hello! Is anybody there?"

The cottage remained dark and unresponsive. A

smell of must and damp plaster came at him in waves from the hallway.

"Call again," said Bonny. "Call *louder*."

He called again, louder, "Is anybody there?" But he knew that he was wasting his breath. The place was empty. He straightened up and turned to Bonny, pinch-faced and tense at his side. "I suppose they were expecting you?" A silly question. No one would make a journey half the length of England purely on the off chance of finding someone at home. "I mean, you did tell them you were coming?"

Bonny's finger went to her mouth. "I thought they'd be in."

"You mean—" For just a moment he was thrown. He had known that *he* was capable of behaving with lunatic irresponsibility, for his father had told him so often enough. He had never expected to meet someone else who did.

"They're *always* in," said Bonny, "always!"

Well, they obviously weren't in now. The thought occurred to Richard: was this how his father felt when confronted with him?

"I take it they do still live here?" he said.

Her head jerked up. She set her jaw defiantly. "Of course they still live here! What d'you mean, do they still live here? They've just gone out for the evening, that's all!"

"The floorboards are up." Richard had bent down and was peering through the flap of the letter box. By standing slightly to one side he could just dimly make out part of the interior. "There's a great gaping hole."

"*What?*" Bonny sprang forward.

He moved aside to let her see. "Are you sure they haven't sold it or something?"

"They wouldn't! They wouldn't do a thing like that! Not without telling me! They're not that sort of people!" Anyone else, but not Nobby and Bo. They were different. She knew they were!

Richard stepped back a pace, looking more closely at the cottage adjoining. That, too, had an air of desolation. One of the windows was broken, and a pile of rubble lay on the path.

"When did you last hear from them?"

"Christmas! I heard from them at Christmas!"

They had sent her a money order and told her to "buy yourself something nice" with it. She had gone straight out and spent it on a present for Jake.

"Christmas is almost three months ago," said Richard.

"Yes. Well . . ." She'd kept meaning to call, it was just that somehow she'd never got around to it, and then the telephone had been cut off because nobody had bothered paying the bill and the one at work was only for emergencies and all the public ones seemed to have been vandalized and—

She looked up again at the silent cottage. "They wouldn't!" she said. "They wouldn't, they wouldn't!" There was a note almost of panic in her voice. She turned and began to hammer on the door with both fists clenched. "They promised me! They told me! They said I could always come here, they said they would always be here, they said, they *said*!"

Richard glanced nervously over his shoulder. This was frightful. Half the road would be out in a second, demanding to know what was going on. He tried to

40

keep calm and imagine how Jan would handle such a situation.

"Why don't we . . ." Suddenly it came to him: "Why don't we try asking someone?"

Bonny hiccuped rather aggressively. "Asking who? *What*?"

"The neighbors, other people. See if they can tell us anything. They might have left a forwarding address." He was pleased with himself for thinking of that. It was obvious; it was sensible.

Bonny, however, seemed less than impressed. "So what if they have?"

"Well, then you'd know where they were."

"I don't want to know where they are!" She had come, and they had not been there. They had moved away, without even telling her. Changed their address and left her to find out from strangers. *She* wasn't going around begging.

"If it's not too far," said Richard, "we might still be able to get down there."

"I don't want to get down there!"

He regarded her helplessly.

"So what *do* you want?"

She wanted Jake. She wanted Nobby and Bo. She wanted to be safely tucked up in bed in her own little cubbyhole of a room, with the roof that sloped down to the floor. They had said that it would always be hers. And now they had gone, without even taking the trouble to say good-bye. They had turned out just the same as everyone else.

"I mean . . ." Richard spread his hands. "What would you suggest?"

41

"Anything! Nothing! I don't care! I don't care any-more!"

This was getting them nowhere. Bonny was in a state, and he was proving himself to be just as useless as he always was. It was time to take a stand.

"I'll tell you what we'll do," he said. "We'll go and have something to eat."

"What with?" She scowled at him resentfully. "We haven't any money."

"I have. I've got my checkbook." He also had his overdraft, huge and rapidly mounting, but like Bonny he had reached the stage where he didn't care. They had eaten nothing all day except soggy toast and filthy cardboard sandwiches filled with strips of plastic. He wasn't driving another yard until he'd put something into his stomach.

The decision made him masterful. "Come!" Without giving himself time to become unmasterful again, he seized hold of Bonny's hand and marched her back off down the road. "Here we are." Firmly he brought her to a halt outside the front entrance of the hotel on the corner. The Albion, it was called.

Bonny plucked agitatedly at his sleeve as he started up the steps. "We can't go in there!"

"Why can't we?"

"In *there*?"

"Why not? We're perfectly respectable." It wasn't as if he had long hair or a beard, or anything that marked him as a danger to society.

"They'll never even let us through the doors," said Bonny.

"You want to bet?"

Indifferent to the ill-bred stares of various guests

dotted about the entrance hall, he led the way across the red-carpeted floor through double swing doors into a cavernous dining room, all bepotted with palms and filled with the muted tinkling of cutlery and glassware. Bonny, clinging nervously to his sleeve, hissed, "I don't like it!"

It was too late to start not liking it. Already a poker-faced waiter was ushering them to a table, Bonny's oversize coat being borne away to the cloakroom with as much reverence as if it were a mink stole.

"There you are, you see." Richard nodded at her. He felt at home in this vast pillared establishment. It was the sort of place his mother had taken them to for morning coffee, or as an occasional treat for lunch, when as children they had accompanied her on shopping expeditions into Cheltenham. "All quite simple."

Yes, but what about afterward? She mouthed it at him, across the table. *When they come around with the bill?*

"We take to our heels and go like the wind." He had never suggested such a thing in his life before. A great glowing spirit of freedom entered into his soul. Suddenly he was feeling like God. He picked up the menu and passed it to her. "Just take a look at that," he said, "and tell me what you want. . . ."

An hour later they were still sitting there. Bonny had consumed one shrimp cocktail with brown bread and butter, scampi in garlic sauce with sautéed potatoes and a green salad, an enormous chunk of sticky strawberry *gâteau* and a cup of coffee with four pieces of Turkish delight (Richard's as well as her own). In addition to the coffee she had drunk one glass of Campari, half a bottle of wine, and a glass of something

called sambuca, which she had chosen because she had
seen someone else drinking it and it looked pretty, with
a little blue flame dancing on the top.

"This is great," she said. She smiled owlishly at
Richard across the table. "D'you always live like this?"

"Only when I can't afford it." He wondered what
state his overdraft was at. A hundred pounds? Two
hundred? He could never pay it back in a month of
Sundays. If his old man were to see him now . . .

"What's the blue flame like?"

Bonny screwed up her nose. "Horrible. Like aniseed
balls. C'n I have something else—take the taste away?"

One hundred pounds, two hundred pounds—what
did he care?

"C'n I have one of those red ones?"

"Cherry brandy?" He looked at her, suddenly uncertain. "You'll get drunk if you're not careful."

She tilted her chin; a familiar gesture. "So what?"

So she didn't look old enough, that was what. She
didn't even look as old as his sister Kate. Kate was
sixteen last August. He leaned forward.

"How old are you?"

Fiercely, she said, "What's that got to do with it?"

Everything. All he needed was to be accused of ab-
duction. That on top of everything else.

Bonny faced him brazenly. "If you must know, I'm
nineteen."

She couldn't be nineteen. He wasn't even nineteen
himself.

"Eighteen?" said Bonny.

No way.

"All right, then! *Six*teen. And if you don't believe
that—" She heaved her canvas bag onto the table, up-

ended it, and shook vigorously. A thick paperback copy of *Forever Amber* fell out with a thud, quickly followed by a cascade of undergarments and a pair of fluffy pink bedroom slippers adorned with woolly bobbles. *"There."*

She thrust a sheet of paper under his nose. It appeared to be a birth certificate. He had just time to see *Father: Unknown* before she snatched it back again.

"Now c'n I have one?"

He shrugged a shoulder. What did it matter if she did get drunk? What did it matter if his overdraft did soar to heights unimaginable? He might just as well owe a thousand as a hundred. He called back the waiter and duly ordered Bonny her cherry brandy.

"Aren't you having one?" she said.

"Couldn't drive if I drank anything else."

She chewed at a fingernail. "Where we driving to?"

"Where did you want to drive to?"

"Don't know."

To his horror, great tears suddenly welled up in her eyes. *Splish splosh* they went, dripping onto the undergarments. He watched them as they fell. A sense of desperation filled him. What was she crying for?

"Do you want me to take you back up to Crewe?"

She shook her head angrily, the short chestnut curls bounding and bobbing, tears spraying her face.

"I can if you like."

"Don't want you to!" She clawed up a pair of frilly underpants and wiped at her eyes with them. Then she gave a loud snuffly sniff and brushed the back of her hand across her nose. "I'll be all right. You don't have to worry about *me.*"

Nevertheless, it seemed to him, he couldn't just

45

abandon her. And anyway, where would he go if he did?

"I've had an idea," he said. Carefully he pushed back his chair and stood up. The room swayed slightly as he did so, but he thought it was more from tiredness than from drink. "Don't run away, I'll be right back."

Bonny watched him cross the restaurant and go out through the double doors. Dimly, without much interest, she wondered if she would ever see him again.

The waiter arrived with her glass of red stuff. She forced herself to keep calm and remain in her seat. He'd probably only gone to the john, and even if he hadn't, so what? They couldn't force her to pay. It wasn't her fault if he'd taken them for a ride. They ought to be more careful who they let into their hotels.

She would give him five minutes, and if he hadn't returned by then she was getting out. No point sitting here like an idiot. She picked up her glass and sniffed at it suspiciously. It smelled like cough medicine.

She didn't care if it was cough medicine. *She* wasn't paying for it.

The clerk behind the reception desk shook his head when Richard asked for two single rooms for the night. They could let him have a double with twin beds, but there wasn't a single left in the whole of the hotel.

Tonight, he didn't care.

"That'll do," he said.

He had already defied his old man, walked out of the parental home, run up an overdraft; now he was going to spend the night sleeping in the same room as a girl he didn't know from Adam—Eve. So what? as Bonny herself would no doubt say.

46

He returned with determined tread to the dining room. As he pushed open the doors he saw a small figure in a pink sweater and a long billowy skirt, with a canvas bag trailing a pair of tights slung over one shoulder, weaving to and fro among the tables toward him.

He was just in time to catch it as it fell.

6
Chapter

When Bonny woke up next morning, she couldn't at first remember where she was. She lay quite still for a moment, with her eyes closed and her hands crossed over her chest. She felt like a big, heavy body suspended in space. Neither sinking nor floating; just suspended.

Carefully she opened her eyes and turned her head on the pillow to see casement windows with curtains pulled back and strange shapes, like crumpled faces, rampaging across the walls. The crumpled faces gradually dissolved, reassembled themselves, and became pale pink roses against a background of straw. Horrible. She closed her eyes again.

Last night she had been drunk, and now she had a

hangover. She supposed it was a hangover. "Head like an old boiler, mouth like a dunghill": that was the way Jake had always described it.

Jake wasn't here anymore; Jake had gone to Dublin. Hot tears filled her aching eyes. She wasn't going to think about Jake.

Somewhere outside a clock began to strike. She lay, listening and counting. Nine o'clock. Ten o'clock. *Eleven.* Even Donovan and Julie might be out of bed by now.

She raised herself on one elbow *(boom* went the old boiler; *blurp* went her stomach). She was still wearing her skirt and sweater, but someone had removed her boots; she could see them, neatly placed side by side, over in the far corner of the room. Her canvas bag, she was relieved to note, was hanging by its strap from the wardrobe door, though there was no sign of her coat. Maybe whoever had taken her boots off for her had hung the coat inside the wardrobe.

The question was, who?

Him?

A few feet away was a second bed. It had obviously been slept in, for the quilt was rumpled and one of the pillows was on the floor. She eyed it dubiously. On the small table that stood between the beds lay a sheet of paper. Gingerly *(sloop* went her stomach; *bang* went her head) she leaned over to get it. It looked as though it was the back cover from a checkbook. A brief message had been scribbled: *Bonny, Have gone out, will be back soon. Call down for anything you want. Richard.*

So it *had* been him. Forgetting the steam hammers she scrambled out of bed and bunnyhopped across to the wardrobe.

Empty.

Where was her coat?

Suddenly she remembered. It had been borne away to some secret place: the poker-faced waiter had insisted. He had wanted to take her canvas bag as well, but she had had sense enough to hang on to that. She wished now that she had hung on to the coat. She didn't like people taking her things away and putting them where she couldn't get at them: it reminded her too much of the children's home.

Slowly her gaze roved the room. No trace of any of *his* stuff. He surely must have had some? He must have. It wasn't normal for people to go driving about, here, there, and everywhere—all over the country— without even so much as a clean pair of underwear. He must have had *something*. In the trunk, perhaps. A suitcase or a holdall.

But then, if he had had a suitcase or a holdall, why had he not brought them into the hotel with him? And if he had brought them into the hotel, why were they not here now?

She went over to the window and knelt on the ledge. Outside was a parking lot. There were about a dozen cars parked there, but the little black VW was not one of them.

He had run out on her. She had thought last night when he left the dining room that he was going to jump into his car and drive off. Now he had actually done it: gone off without paying—leaving *her* behind as a decoy.

Bonny chewed in vexation at a jagged edge of fingernail. She had been right from the word go: he was nothing but a con man. She ought to have known bet-

50

ter than to let herself be taken in by him. Stupid cow! She could hear Jake saying it.

Angrily, before self-pity could engulf her, she bounced herself back off the window ledge. She had to get out of this place. *Out,* before they started asking questions. The only problem was how.

She stood awhile, gnawing at her fingernail. No point going down the stairs and through the main entrance; that would be asking for trouble. They were bound to have figured out by now that something was up. Probably, if she did but know it, there were guards posted outside the very door.

Thoughtfully she turned back again to the window. She had climbed out of windows before now; that would be nothing new. With one ear cocked in the direction of the door she eased up the latch and put her head out. The parking lot, one floor below, seemed deserted. There was another window to her left, but that was firmly closed. To her right . . .

A drainpipe. That settled it: the window was the way to go.

On cautious tiptoe she went back across the room and unhooked her bag from the wardrobe door. It was a nuisance about her coat. It was the only one she'd got, but she didn't dare risk going downstairs and finding out what had happened to it.

For just a moment her courage faltered. The sky outside was black and threatening. It was going to come down but good, and she without a coat to her back or a penny to her name; and worse, far worse, than all besides, without the least idea of where to go, or of what to do when she got there.

She tilted her chin. So what? She had had it too easy

51

these last few years with Nobby and Bo. She had known all along it couldn't last. They weren't like real parents. Real parents put up with you no matter what, even if you did forget to call for months on end. They didn't just up and go off without telling you. People with real parents always had a place to go.

Well, she didn't have real parents, so that was that. She didn't have them and she didn't want them and she didn't *care*. All she wanted to do now was get out.

As she opened the window an old yellow post office van was entering the parking lot. She watched in silent irritation as it drove slowly across, pulling up almost directly beneath her. That was just marvelous. That was just what she wanted. Some idiot in a van parking in a spot where he could hardly fail to catch sight of her.

The idiot in the van opened the driver's door and began to get out. Swiftly Bonny drew back, wrapping herself in one of the curtains for cover. She would count to a hundred, and if he hadn't gone by then . . .

If he hadn't gone by then, she would just have to take her chance.

Richard's immediate thought, as he opened the door of the hotel bedroom, was that Bonny had gone. It was a second or so before he located her, over by the windows, huddled in the folds of the curtain, peering out at him like a startled leprechaun.

"It's only me," he said, in case she had thought it was going to be someone else. It was the only reason he could think of for her to be huddled in a curtain.

She emerged fretfully. "Where have you been?"

"I just popped out," he said, "to get some money."

52

"So where's the car?"

"I sold it."

"You *sold* it?" Her eyes widened accusingly. "Sold the *car?*"

"I had to. It was the only way I could raise any cash."

"So how much'd you get?"

"They gave me five fifty, part exchange."

"You're joking!"

"I'm not."

"Five *fifty?*"

"Yes." He had thought it was rather good. He had been feeling quite proud of himself.

"So what did they palm you off with?"

"A van. It's quite reasonable, it—"

"A *van?*" She turned, unbelieving, to the window. "That heap of crap?"

"It's better than it looks. They're quite sturdy, these post office jobs."

Bonny shook her head. That anyone could be that *gullible.* "You should've told me," she said. "You should've taken me with you." She wouldn't have let them rook him like that. Some people just weren't safe let out by themselves. "Too trusting," she said, "that's your trouble."

"I don't quite see what else I could have done."

"*I'*d have done something, don't you worry!"

She probably would. Crestfallen, all pleasure gone, he tossed his new set of keys onto the nearest bed. "Have you had any breakfast yet?" he asked her.

"No." She hadn't had a chance to think about breakfast; though now that she *did* . . .

53

"I'll call down for some. What would you like? Eggs? Bacon? Cereal?"

Now that she did, it didn't seem to her that it was too advisable. In fact she rather thought—

"I'm going to be sick!"

Richard found himself suddenly thrust to one side as Bonny, hand pressed to her mouth, charged blindly for the door. He had just sufficient presence of mind to call after her as she blundered past, "Third on the left!"

He hoped she made it in time. It would be very embarrassing if she didn't. It had been somewhat embarrassing last night, in the restaurant, except that last night he had been in a mood of mad rashness and so it hadn't really bothered him. This morning when he woke up he had known at once that he was back to normal—in other words, useless, spineless, and introspective. The only difference was that this morning, unlike other mornings, he had determined to do something about it. And he *had* done something about it. He had gone out and sold the car; and that was still an achievement even if Bonny quite plainly did think he'd allowed himself to be conned. In any case, he was by no means certain that she was right. They'd thrown in the van, hadn't they? And while it mightn't be much to look at, it was undeniably transport. He wasn't *completely* stupid.

To prove the point he called down for breakfast. Breakfast, he was informed, had finished over an hour ago. Nothing daunted, he ordered a pot of coffee and a plate of muffins. It was probably as much as Bonny could cope with in her present state.

The coffee came, Bonny did not. He was just about

54

to nerve himself to go and look for her when she reappeared. He studied her anxiously. "Are you okay?"

"I've just been sick." She announced it with relish, as if being sick were a matter for self-congratulation. *"Four times."*

"You'd better have some coffee."

"Ugh!" She shuddered elaborately. "I couldn't!"

"You ought, if you've been sick. It'll do you good." Suddenly he felt himself becoming masterful again. "Here!" He picked up the coffee cup and thrust it at her. "Take it!"

To his amazement she did. Wonders would never cease. Jauntily he helped himself to a muffin and broke it in two. "So where shall we go next?"

She regarded him broodingly over the rim of the cup. "Where're you going?"

"I can go wherever you want me to go. If you'd like me to take you back up to Crewe—"

"I don't want to go back up to Crewe!"

He hoped she wasn't going to burst into tears again. That really *would* embarrass him. He never knew which way to look when his mother broke down and started crying, which she quite frequently did.

"What about your job?" he said.

"What job?"

"With the theater."

"Oh! That's finished. They don't employ you forever."

"So what will you do?"

She shrugged a shoulder. "Dunno. Thumb a lift, see where it takes me. Get another job. Find somewhere to bed down. Can't tell till it happens, can I?"

He supposed that if she really *were* an actress she

55

couldn't. He wondered what it must be like, leading such a precarious existence. Part of him—the old, spineless, couldn't-say-boo-to-a-goose part—shied away from it. The other part—the new, bold, go-any-where-do-anything part—was almost drawn to the idea.

"When you say get another job," he said, "d'you mean in the theater, or—"

"Anywhere. These days, you're lucky to *get* a job. Not much point being fussy."

"So where's the best place to start looking?"

"London," said Bonny.

"So perhaps I should take you to London?"

"Can if you want." What was his game? Take her here, take her there—what was he *after*? "Don't have to if you don't want to. I can always hitch another lift."

He frowned. "You oughtn't to do that sort of thing."

"Why not?"

"It's dangerous. Any pervert could stop and pick you up."

"Like you, I s'pose."

Yes. Absolutely. He looked down at the pieces of broken muffin still in his hand.

"Here, I was only joking!" said Bonny.

She might be. His old man wasn't.

"Drink your coffee," he said. "It'll get cold."

With surprising meekness she did. She obviously felt that she had upset him and wanted to make amends.

She hadn't upset him. From now on he wasn't going to *let* himself be upset. He was going to be tough and independent. Go his own way, do his own thing. He took off his glasses and peered around shortsightedly for something to wipe them on.

"D'you really want to come to London?" said Bonny.

"Why not?" If that was the place where one got work. He suddenly saw himself stripped to the waist, bronzed and muscle-bound, heaving bricks on a building site. That would be something to tell Jan.

"All right!" Bonny suddenly banged down her coffee cup and sprang up. "If we're going to go, then let's *go!*"

7
Chapter

It was after midday by the time they left Southampton, the reason being that the van wouldn't start. On the whole Bonny was quite restrained about it, contenting herself with the comment that it was "just as well we didn't need to make a quick getaway."

She didn't seem to be in such a prattling mood as she had been yesterday; indeed she struck him as rather subdued. He didn't know whether it was the aftereffects of being sick or she was brooding over the old ladies. He tried a tentative inquiry—"Are you all right?"—but she just glared at him and said, *"Me? I'm* all right." He sought for something else.

"When we actually get there—London, that is"— was the engine really misfiring or was it just his imagination?—"what do we have to do?"

58

"What d'you mean, what do we have to do?"

"Well, about work. Where do we start looking? Employment agencies?"

"Employment agencies!" Bonny uttered the words scornfully. "Fat lot of use they are." She didn't say why they were a fat lot of use; humbly he accepted the fact. "Look in the papers, that's the best thing."

"What about somewhere to live?" He and Jan had gone to a real estate agent, but that had been in Bristol. Things might be different in London. "What's the usual procedure?"

Bonny shrugged.

"Ask around, find digs." It was the way Jake had done it, up in Crewe. "You just go around to places. Cafés and—" She was about to say pubs but, remembering the state of her head when she woke up that morning, decided to cross pubs off the list. "Clubs and things, where you can meet people. There's always something going on." Jake hadn't had any difficulty. He'd struck up a conversation with Julie and Donovan the very first night.

"Where did you live when you were at RADA?"

"Here and there." Bonny twisted her head to peer into the recesses of the van. "I s'pose we could always sleep in the back if we had to. Just for a night or two. Until we found somewhere. I mean, it's got to be about two o'clock *now*. All that messing around . . . Can't we go any faster? Carry on at this rate, it'll be midnight before we get there."

At least if it had been midnight they would have had the place to themselves. As it was they arrived in the middle of the homeward rush, four thirty in the afternoon and all the roads a heaving mass of traffic. Richard found himself buffeted along in the midst of it with no quarter given, no allowances made. Only let him pause for a fraction of a second to consider which direction he should take and instant cacophony broke loose, every horn within a ten-mile radius angrily blaring out a protest. Even Bonny, who was supposed to be familiar with the place, seemed infected by the general lunacy and kept screaming at him to "Go down there, go down there!" or "Right! right! make a right!" After she had twice screamed "Right!" when there was no right turn and twice attempted to send him the wrong way down a one-way street, he began to have a suspicion that she had no more idea than he which way they were headed.

"I thought you'd lived here?" he said.

"Not *here*," said Bonny. "I didn't live *here*."

"Where, then?"

"Piccadilly Circus," said Bonny.

"Right. So how do we get there?"

Silence.

"Look, there's a traffic circle coming up," said Richard. "Which lane am I—"

"That one! That one! Over there!"

Going around the traffic circle for the second time— the first time around he missed his exit and couldn't get out—he was sworn at by a cabdriver. Bonny promptly rolled down the window, stuck out her head, and swore back.

"You just shut your fat mouth!"

He wished she wouldn't, particularly as the fault had been his. "I cut the guy off, coming around that corner. I should have been farther over."

"So what? You didn't do it on purpose. He doesn't

60

have to go bawling at you. You want to stand up for yourself."

Shades of Kate: *You ought to stand up to him.*

"I do," he said, "when I'm in the right."

"You don't," said Bonny. "You're not aggressive enough. You let them push you around all the time. Like back there, with that truck. It was your right of way; why didn't you take it?"

Basically because he hadn't fancied the idea of being crushed to death. For one thing, his mother wouldn't like it; neither would Jan—always assuming, after receiving that card, that Jan still cared. He glanced at Bonny, sitting all hunched up and purse-lipped in her seat, like a little angry dwarf.

"Are you sure we're going the right way?"

"Don't know till I see a sign. I told you, I didn't *live* in this part. It's not that easy."

She could say that again.

They drove for a while in silence, carried along by the traffic.

"That was Gower Street!" said Richard.

Bonny looked at him crossly. "So what?"

"Isn't that where RADA is?" He was sure it was where RADA was. He remembered Philip Russell telling him "near the British Museum." "Your old drama school," he said.

Bonny pressed her face to the window.

"I didn't go to that bit. I went to another bit. Why don't you turn down here?"

He didn't turn down there for the simple reason that it was signposted CITY & EAST, and even he knew that what they wanted was the West End. He was beginning

61

to wonder about Bonny. He wasn't too sure that she always told the truth.

He recognized Piccadilly Circus, when at last they reached it, by the statue of Eros. He said to Bonny, "Look, there's Eros."

"There's what?" said Bonny.

She *couldn't* have lived in Piccadilly Circus and not know Eros. As a matter of fact, Piccadilly Circus didn't look to him at all the sort of place where a student was likely to have lived. It was all stores and movie theaters and big glassy office blocks.

"Well, I didn't mean Piccadilly Circus it*self,*" said Bonny. She said it as if it had been ridiculous of him ever to suppose that she had. "I meant *near . . . near* Piccadilly Circus."

"So where shall we try?"

"Over there." She pointed. "Up that road there."

With some misgivings he followed her directions. There wasn't any parking space in the road she had indicated, but he found a spot not too far off, up a side street. The first thing to catch his eye as he stepped onto the sidewalk was a sign that said CINDY'S, with a picture of a well-endowed woman not wearing very much clothing. A little farther was another sign that said STRIP DU MONDE, with an illuminated hand pointing to a basement doorway.

"What we want," said Bonny, "is somewhere we can sit down and talk to people."

"Yes."

They walked on. LAS PALMAS. CAROUSEL. NAKED CITY—

"This'll do," said Bonny.

He looked at her, startled. Naked City?

"Not *there*," said Bonny. "That's a dance hall!"

Richard eyed it dubiously. It didn't look to him like a dance hall.

"Course it is," said Bonny. "What d'you think it is?"

He didn't like to say what he thought it was. In any case, he could be wrong; he hadn't had much experience in these matters—he hadn't had *any* experience in these matters. He was beginning to think that Bonny hadn't, either.

She led the way into a rather sleazy-looking sandwich bar with Formica-topped tables and encrusted bottles of HP sauce. At four thirty in the afternoon there weren't many people in there, just one lone woman smoking a cigarette, an olive-skinned man wearing dark glasses, and a couple of youths sitting close together in a corner. Richard glanced at the youths and quickly glanced away again. Bonny jerked at his sleeve.

"Try asking *him*." She nodded at a fat man behind the counter.

"Asking him what?"

"If he knows anywhere we can get a room!"

"All right." He wished Bonny would do it herself since it was her idea, but he knew that was only being cowardly. One thing about his old man, he never shirked his duty. He supposed, in the circumstances, that it *was* his duty. For all their talk about sexual equality, it still seemed to be the man's job to take the lead. "D'you want something to eat?"

"Bacon," said Bonny. "In a sandwich. And a cup of tea—a *huge* one."

She watched as Richard walked up to the counter.

63

The back of his neck had gone all red. She wondered if he could be trusted to ask properly—or even to ask at all. She should have done it herself; it was always best to do things yourself. It was the only way you could be sure of getting them done. She bet he wouldn't do it.

Richard half turned with two mugs of tea. As he did so, the woman with the cigarette leaned forward and said something to him. Bonny observed with interest the color deepening on his face. That was one of the disadvantages of having fair skin: when you were embarrassed, it showed. Jake's skin had been sallow, and usually covered with a three-day growth of beard. He could have blushed to the roots of his hair and no one would be any the wiser. But then it was hard to imagine Jake ever *being* embarrassed.

Richard was smiling now and backing away. It was a nervous sort of smile, and his face had gone bright scarlet. Bonny felt almost sorry for him. She went up to the counter to collect the sandwiches.

"Did my friend ask you if you knew anywhere we might be able to get rooms?"

"He did." A plate was slapped down in front of her. "And I don't."

"Oh. Well—thank you very much." And the same to you. Affronted, Bonny snatched up the plate and marched back with it. She had always heard that Londoners were rude and unpleasant; now she knew it. Nobody had behaved like that up in Crewe.

"I asked him," said Richard. "He didn't know anywhere."

"I know he didn't. What did *she* want?"

"Nothing very much."

"So what was she talking to you about?"

64

"She was just . . . being friendly."

"Oh?"

"If you must know," said Richard, "she wanted to offer me a bed for the night."

"*You?*"

"Yes."

"Why only you? Why not both of us?"

Richard gave her a pained look.

"Oh, I *see*," said Bonny. "You mean she's a"—she mouthed the word, silently—*prostitute.*

Richard's blush came back in full force. "Not necessarily."

"Course she is!" Bonny turned and studied her. "Sticks out a mile." She munched for a bit on her bacon sandwich. It wasn't anywhere near as good as the bacon sandwiches she'd had up in Crewe. She turned her attention to the man in dark glasses. "P'raps I should try asking him."

"I don't think you ought," said Richard.

"Why not?"

Because he looked like something out of the Mafia, that was why not.

"Never get anywhere if you don't ask," said Bonny.

If anyone was going to ask, it ought to be him. He knew that it ought to be him. He chewed rather hard on a cheese and tomato sandwich that tasted like blotting paper. Over in the far corner the two youths were sitting very close, side by side, their shoulders touching. One had a cap of bright gold hair, molded perfectly to his head; the other was wearing an earring. He wasn't sure, but he rather thought they were holding hands beneath the table. Suddenly the boy with the earring looked up and caught Richard's eye. He smiled. Caught off guard, Richard smiled back. At his side, Bonny giggled.

"Get her!"

Richard turned his eyes away. "Sorry?"

"Boys in the band," said Bonny. "Them." She nodded her head. "Queer."

Richard looked down at his blotting paper sandwich. The cheese was hard and yellow, like a strip of plastic. He pushed it away.

"You oughtn't to call people that. It's not polite."

"Oh, well! Gay, then." She pulled a face. "It's all the same."

It wasn't all the same. He risked another quick glance across the room. This time the other boy looked up; his gaze was cold and hostile.

"Poufs," said Bonny.

This was too much. He scraped back his chair.

"Let's go!"

Bonny, clutching her canvas bag and still swallowing the remains of her bacon sandwich, scuttled out indignantly after him onto the sidewalk.

"What'd you do that for?"

"I don't think this is the sort of area we ought to be looking in."

"Why not? What's wrong with it? Just because you saw a couple of gays?"

"No." He set off abruptly up the road. "Let's go somewhere else."

"Where?"

Anywhere Bonny wasn't going to be tempted to make offensive remarks. He quickened his pace, anxious to be gone. Bonny gave a little skip to catch up.

"Where?"

"Kensington." He had once had a great-aunt who lived in Kensington. He had vague childhood memories of visiting her there. There had been a park—Kensington Gardens?—and lots of big houses.

"It'll be dark before we know it," said Bonny. There was a definite grumble in her voice. "If we don't find somewhere soon—"

"I thought you said we'd have to be prepared to sleep rough for a night or two."

"Yes, but only if we *have* to. There's no point wasting time chasing over half of London."

"We're not chasing over half of London. We've only tried Piccadilly Circus."

"We haven't tried Piccadilly Circus! We've hardly even *started* on Piccadilly Circus. You've only asked one person."

"Well, I'm not asking anymore." Not in this part of the world he wasn't. He'd heard what happened to people who hung around Piccadilly for too long: they ended up in drug dens or houses of vice. He said as much to Bonny, who hooted derisively.

"Houses of vice! What are you talking about?"

"Brothels," said Richard.

"For goodness' sake!" Bonny rolled her eyes. "Don't talk so crazy!"

He wasn't talking crazy; these things happened. He set his jaw stubbornly. Bonny could laugh if she liked: he was not doing anymore asking in this part of the world, and that was that.

With Bonny sulking at his elbow he purchased a map of London from a shop selling miniature Union Jacks and matchboxes with views of St. Paul's, checked their position, and struck out briskly in the

67

direction of the van, Bonny alternately jogging and hopping at his side in an effort to keep up.

"You don't"—jog-hop—"have to *gallop*," she said.

"Sorry." He turned and held out a hand. "Give me your bag."

"I can manage the *bag*. Just don't *run*."

Kensington, which they found quite easily now that he had his street map, was just as he remembered from his visit as a child. Now that he saw it again he could quite clearly recall walking through the park with Sue and his parents, and Kate in her stroller. Sue had got into trouble, behaving like a tomboy, climbing up a tree, and he had disgraced himself getting his feet wet in a pond, trying to reach a toy boat that another boy had been sailing. Great-aunt Dot had lived in a cottage nearby.

"This it?" said Bonny. She looked sniffily out of the van window. "Not going to find anywhere in a place like this."

He was nettled. How did she know? At least it wasn't riddled with Strips du Monde and Naked Cities.

"Not a chance," said Bonny. "Too posh."

By nine thirty in the evening they had moved on from the posh area into a dismal hinterland of crumbling Victorian mansions and boarded-up shops, which Bonny said was "more like it." They had worked their way there by degrees, drinking so many cups of tea and coffee, eating so many blotting paper sandwiches, talking to so many total strangers, that Richard was beginning to feel quite worn out, both physically and mentally. Bonny, on the other hand, was still bright-eyed and alert, even though it was she who had done all the talking. While Richard stood dithering, nerving him-

68

self to say something, Bonny just went ahead and said it: " 'Scuse me, d'you happen to know of any rooms anywhere about?" Unfortunately, nobody ever did.

"Do you really think," said Richard, "that we're going about this in the right way?" He didn't like to say what he really meant, which was that he'd had enough and wanted to give in, wanted to spend the night hibernating in a hotel and never mind what it cost, just so long as he could have a hot bath and sleep in a proper bed and not have to keep talking to people. "You don't think we ought to call it a day and have a rethink in the morning?"

"Let's try somewhere different," said Bonny. "Let's try over there."

He looked where she was pointing.

"An amusement arcade?"

"Why not?"

His old man had always said that amusement arcades were the scum of the earth. He had said that more petty crimes took place in amusement arcades than almost anywhere else.

"C'mon!" Bonny wielded him a blow with her canvas bag, from which she still obstinately refused to be parted. "Stop being so fuddy-duddy. Got 'ny change?"

"What do you want change for?"

"The machines! You can't go into an amusement arcade and not have a *little* go at it. Just five minutes, that's all."

Resigned, he passed over a handful of loose coins and at Bonny's insistence went off with a five-pound note to get more.

"Just stay put," he said. "And *don't talk* to anyone."

"All right."

He was only gone for a few minutes. When he got back, Bonny had disappeared. His first reaction was one of extreme irritation: he had told her to stay *put*; his second, one of panic at being left by himself. Then he turned and saw her. She was coming toward him, a big beam of triumph on her face.

"I've found somewhere!"

He was instantly suspicious. "How?"

"I asked this boy. I saw him st—"

"You've been talking to people!"

"Yes, well, I saw him standing there, so I—"

"I thought I told you not to. Not without me!"

"Well, but you never *say* anything. Anyway, it doesn't matter any more 'cause I've found somewhere."

Now that she had, he wasn't at all sure he wanted to go there.

"Where is it?"

"Just up the road; it's a condemned building."

"Sounds iffy."

"What d'you mean, sounds iffy?"

"Well . . . a squat." He'd never envisaged them doing anything illegal, and he was pretty sure that squatting *was* illegal. He'd heard his old man going on about it often enough.

"What's the matter with you?" Bonny was looking at him angrily. "I spend all these hours talking to people while you just trail along moaning; then when I find somewhere you say it sounds *iffy*. What'd you want? A room at Buckingham Palace?"

He'd been thinking more along the lines of a bed for the night at the nearest hotel, then stopping at a real estate agency as he and Jan had done, but he knew if he said so it would only rouse Bonny's contempt. He didn't like it when she looked at him with her lips all scrunched up tight and her eyes radiating scorn. He made one last feeble attempt at asserting himself.

"So who is this boy?"

"His name's Vic."

"Yes, but who *is* he?"

"I don't know who he is! Owns the place, that's all I know."

"How can you own it?"

"Well, runs it, then!" Bonny was obviously starting to lose patience. "It's the same thing. He's the one that's in charge, the one who says who can go there. *I*'m going there."

Richard could do what he liked: Bonny was going there whether he went or not. He felt a momentary hurt, almost a sense of betrayal. After all they had been through together Bonny could just walk off and not care.

"This is him now," said Bonny.

Richard looked up. A boy dressed in baggy jeans and a thick, army green sweater was pushing his way toward them. He was about the same age as Richard, several inches shorter but a good deal stockier. He jerked his head at Bonny.

"Okay?"

Bonny hesitated. She looked back at Richard. "So are you coming, or not?"

"Oh, I suppose . . . if you really insist . . ."

"Suit yourself," said Vic.

"No, that's all right." Bonny slipped her hand into Richard's. "He's coming."

71

8
Chapter

"The thing is—" Bonny knelt on her mattress, combing the tangles out of her hair—"it's no use looking for something that's going to need references and things." Miss Amphlett would never give her a reference in a month of Sundays, or if she did it would be a stinker: *In my experience Miss McEvoy is totally untrustworthy and not to be relied upon. She is unpunctual, slovenly, slapdash, and disobedient; altogether a thoroughly bad influence. . . .* "The sort of jobs that ask for references, they're the sort that take ages considering you. What we want is something *immediate.* Course, there might be a bit of trouble about cards. They always ask you for your cards." Hers were still with Miss Amphlett up in Crewe. It would perhaps be safer to say that she had lost them. By the time they found out, it would almost certainly be time to be moving on. She couldn't imagine staying in the same job for more than a few weeks: she would go mad. She looked across at Richard. "You got yours on you?"

Richard paused in the act of cleaning his glasses. He peered at her shortsightedly. "My what?"

"Your cards."

"I don't think I've got any cards."

"Haven't got any *cards*?"

"Well—" He hesitated. "What cards are you talking about?"

"*Cards*. For *tax*. Haven't you ever worked?" He couldn't have done; if he had he would know about cards. Where had he *been*? Bonny stuffed her hairbrush down the side of her bag.

"Let's go up the road and get a paper. See what's going on."

"All right."

Richard settled his glasses back on his nose. His glasses at least were clean, which was more than could be said for the rest of him. He hadn't been able to have a hot bath, or even a hot splash, because the house that Vic had brought them to was officially condemned and had been boarded up, which meant that all the services had been cut off. The taps still ran and the toilets still flushed (one of the toilets—the one in the basement, three floors down; the one in the upstairs bathroom had been pulled away from the wall), but there wasn't any means of heating the water except for down in the communal kitchen, where there was an old kerosene stove and a small gas burner of the type Richard remembered from camping holidays in France. You

73

could just about boil a cupful of water on it, or warm up a can of baked beans.

One thing Bonny had neglected to tell him last night was that they would have to share a room; that was something he hadn't bargained for. He wasn't quite sure yet how he felt about it. He knew how he felt about the room itself. It was right at the top of the house, reached by a flight of steep, uncarpeted stairs from the second-floor landing. It must once have been a nursery, for there were still bars at the windows and a large mesh screen in front of the fireplace. Now it was stark and chill, with a worn strip of linoleum laid over bare boards. Someone at some stage had attempted to brighten it up by painting the surrounding area primrose yellow and the walls a deep shade of purple. (Drug addicts, his old man would have said. He was always saying people were drug addicts.) In one corner of the room the rain had come in, leaving a slimy green waterfall effect down the purple wall. The floorboards beneath were wet and spongy and smelled of bad wood, like rotting trees. Someone—the last tenants, the drug addicts?—had left behind a few sticks of furniture: an old kitchen dresser painted blue, a gas stove that looked as if it should be in a museum, and a trundle bed with strange blotches on the mattress. They had split the trundle into two. Richard had taken the bottom half, Bonny the top. She didn't seem too worried about the blotches. As she said, they didn't go all the way through, and at least the mattress was soft, even if it did sag in the middle.

"We'll get some cheap blankets sometime. It'll make it really cozy."

He didn't know about cozy. It seemed appalling to

74

him, but he didn't like to say so. He knew because of reading George Orwell that it was better than a doss house. Maybe when he had been able to buy a toothbrush and some soap and a towel and a change of clothes, he would feel better about it. He had had a moment of deep depression when he woke up that morning. For one treacherous flash he had even felt anger and resentment against Jan for being the cause of his being there. He would be glad to get out into the open and recapture some of that spirit of determination that had buoyed him up at the start of his journey. This was, after all, supposed to be an adventure, was it not? A test of his independence and resourcefulness. He had to get a job and prove himself.

They clattered down the uncarpeted stairs, down two more flights covered in frayed linoleum, along the narrow hallway to the back door, and out into the overgrown yard. From the front the house looked deserted, with boards nailed across the windows and a padlock on the door. Around at the back nobody had bothered. It was a piece of cake, Vic had said, and he winked as he said it.

"Bit of the old B and E."

("What's B and E?" Richard had asked Bonny later. "Breaking and entering," Bonny had said, eyes wide. Imagine not knowing *that*.)

Richard had felt vaguely uneasy ever since. If Vic were the sort of person who didn't mind breaking into houses, then he was probably the sort who wouldn't mind breaking into motor vehicles, either. The post office van mightn't be much, but it was all they'd got. He wouldn't want to lose it.

Out in the street (the van was still there) they bought

a copy of the local paper and took it with them into a nearby café to read over breakfast. Between mouthfuls of bacon and eggs Bonny read aloud from the help wanted columns.

" 'Car cleaners, casual drivers, must be over twenty-one'—*that's* no good. 'Clerical assistant.' You could be a clerical assistant."

"Mm." It wasn't quite what he had had in mind, but as Bonny had said, you couldn't afford to be choosy.

" 'Good at figures.' Are you good at figures?"

"Not really."

"It says good at figures essential. . . . What about clerk-typist? Can you type?"

He shook his head.

"No," said Bonny, "neither can I. Only with one finger. . . . 'Dental nurse, dental receptionist, drivers . . . Must have own four-door sedan'—there you are, you see! If you hadn't gone and got rid of the car—"

"But it was a two door," he said.

"It was still a *car.*" She turned the page. "What about electrician? It says, 'Electrician, own transport—' "

He made a face. He didn't know the first thing about electricity, other than how to change a fuse and put a plug on. Jan said he was pretty stupid even at that.

"All right, then . . . what about 'experienced export clerk, experienced figure clerk, experienced'—why do they all say *experienced?*—'experienced wages clerk, experienced window cleaner'—should've thought *any*one could just clean windows—'full-time sales assistant, fashion boutique, must have previous experience. Full-time sales staff, supermarket chain, experience preferred.' I could try for those."

By the time she had finished her bacon and eggs Bonny had found no less than eight jobs that she could try for. She hadn't found any at all for Richard.

"There's got to be *some*thing." She pushed away her empty plate and spread the paper out across the table. "I mean, what can you actually do?"

What *could* he actually do, when it came down to it? He couldn't type, he couldn't do figures, didn't know anything about electricity—Jan always said that he was worse than useless.

"I mean, apart from medieval history," said Bonny. She looked at him. "You can't get to college without being able to do *some*thing."

He brightened. "I can speak French," he said. "And a bit of Russian."

Bonny ran her eye swiftly down the columns of the paper.

"Can't see anyone who wants someone who can speak French and a bit of Russian. What else can you do?"

"I can ride."

"Ride what? Motorcycle?"

"Horses."

"In *London*? Who's going to want you to ride horses in London?"

Or anywhere else, for that matter.

"Can't you do anything useful? Like . . . 'switchboard operator-receptionist, switchboard operator-typist, switchboard operator—' "

"What about work on a building site?" He suggested it rather shyly. He still cherished these brave, butch visions of himself stripped to the waist, manfully humping hodfuls of bricks with a bright yellow safety helmet on his head. "Couldn't I do that?"

"*Laboring?*" said Bonny. "I thought you were s'posed to have a brain?"

He was, but it didn't seem to be of very much use to anyone. Besides, he wanted to do something that would impress Jan, something dangerous, or daring, or unusual. He didn't just want to sit in an office adding up rows of figures or putting files away. Anybody could do that.

"Here's something." Bonny stabbed a finger down onto the paper. " 'Telephone researchers required, eighteen plus, suitable for students, unemployed actors/actresses, etc. Must have good speaking voice. Apply Personnel Officer, Market Decisions Limited.' You could do that. You've got a good speaking voice, all posh and la-di-da."

He winced. Was that really how he came across? "Why not you?" he said. "You're an actress."

"I've already found something," said Bonny. She pushed back her chair. "Let's go and get some change and start phoning."

He felt quite nervous, telephoning the personnel officer at Market Decisions. He knew that it was ridiculous, but if it hadn't been for standing in the phone booth listening to Bonny he wouldn't have been able to think what to say. As it was, he obviously managed not to sound too cretinous, for he was given an interview for three o'clock that same afternoon.

"Don't see what you're so surprised about," said Bonny. "They said good speaking voices, didn't they?"

In preparation for the interview he went into the nearest department store and stocked up with all the things he should have brought with him from home, had he only stopped to think about it at the time, which of course he hadn't, being in too much of a state. Back in the house he boiled up a pan of water on the gas burner, carried it up to the top floor, carefully washed and shaved, brushed his teeth, combed his hair, and put on an entire change of clothes. Bonny, who had interviews of her own to go to, sat on her mattress watching him and saying that he was crazy.

"What d'you want to buy *trousers* for? What's wrong with jeans? Ones you had on were okay; all they needed was a bit of a brush. You're potty, going to all that trouble. Job's only a job. 'S not worth it."

Maybe it wasn't, but he had had it dinned into him too often, both at school and at home: "Never get anywhere if you go around looking scruffy." He wouldn't have felt comfortable going to an interview unwashed and unshaven and wearing old jeans. He tried explaining some of this to Bonny, but she just looked at him and shook her head and said again that he was crazy.

The personnel officer at Market Decisions was a lady named Fabia Collins. She looked disturbingly like the wife of his headmaster at school, whom they had irreverently but only half in jest referred to as the Figurehead. The Figurehead hadn't been at all the sort of person to approve of blue jeans (not to mention blue chins) so that on the whole he felt he had been right to stick to his guns and not let Bonny bully him.

He had had only the haziest notion what to expect from a job interview. They'd told them, at school, how to handle interviews for college, but not interviews for jobs. He'd imagined that probably it would go on for about an hour, with searching questions being asked as

79

to which school he'd been to, what exams he'd passed, what subjects he was studying for his degree; but Miss Collins didn't seem particularly interested in anything of that kind. What she seemed mainly interested in was his ability to read from a sheet of paper that she handed to him. She told him that he could take his time—"Read through it first if you want to"—but sight-reading had never held any terrors for him. In fact, he found it easier to read than to be interviewed.

" 'Good afternoon. My name is' Richard Islip 'and I work for Market Decisions Limited, a research organization based in London. We're currently conducting a survey about television advertising, and so that we can represent everybody's point of view we're talking to a wide cross section of the public. May I first of all assure you—' "

At that point Miss Collins reached across the desk, took back the paper, and asked him when he wanted to start. It seemed that he had his first job.

Going back to the house—he couldn't think of it as "home"—he felt a sense of elation. He had actually done it: he had actually found himself work! He raced up the stairs three at a time and threw open the door of the room.

"I've got it!"

Bonny, who was lying on her stomach on her mattress, reading her book about the Plague and the Fire of London, didn't even bother to look up.

"Told you you would."

"Yes, but . . ." She didn't understand. It was his *first job*. The first time he would ever have functioned as a fully paid up, productive member of society. "She asked me when I wanted to start, so I said tomorrow. I thought I might as well. After all, we could do with the bread and—"

"So how much they paying you?"

"I—I don't know." It suddenly struck him: he'd never thought to inquire. "I suppose she must have told me. I can't remember. But she didn't want cards or anything. *Or* references. Apparently it's mainly students; students and theater people. You can choose your own hours, morning or evenings, whatever you want. You can even work Sundays if you want. What you do, you have these questionnaires and you're given a telephone directory and you have to telephone people and ask them things, like what sort of work they do, and how old are they, and which television stations do they normally watch, and what commercials can they remember seeing during the past month—it goes on for pages. It's quite complicated. You have to spend the whole of the first day being trained."

"Sounds okay," said Bonny.

"Yes." He was quite looking forward to it; that was why he had said he would start the next day. "What about you? How did yours go?"

"All right," said Bonny.

"Did you get something?"

She grunted.

"Which one? The fashion one?"

"Supermarket. Fashion one had gone."

"Oh! That's a shame."

"Why?" She looked at him rather fiercely. "What's a shame about it?"

"I don't know, I just thought . . ." He had just thought that a fashion shop sounded more fun than a supermarket, that was all.

"Doesn't make any difference. They're all the same. All boring—all *horrible*." Bonny closed her book with a bang. "People pushing you about, telling you what to do, nagging at you—'slike being in prison. I *hate* it."

He frowned.

"Can't you find something that you don't hate?"

"Like what?"

"Well—" He didn't like to say, like acting. He wouldn't want to embarrass her. She might have forgotten telling him that she was an actress. "Something where people *don't* push you about and tell you what to do and nag at you."

"Aren't any jobs where people don't push you about and nag at you. Not unless you're one of *them*. You just have to put up with it."

That was why Jake hardly ever worked, because he refused to put up with it. That was why he had gone to Ireland to be a folksinger. What would he be doing, right at this minute? Standing in a pub, strumming his guitar? She could see him, in his old patched jeans and his red check shirt, with a yellow scarf tied about his neck and all the women going bananas over him, because that was the effect that Jake had on women. If he had only taken her with him, she wouldn't have to be starting this lousy job on Monday. It would be just the same as Matheson's. Sitting there behind the cash register, taking money, giving change, getting told off for being late, for being rude, for being careless. One lone tear went trickling down her cheek. Jake *could* have taken her with him. He *could*'ve.

Richard stood in silence, all pride in his own achievement temporarily eclipsed. He didn't like to see Bonny so down when he, for once, was so up. He sought in his mind for something to make her happy again.

"Let's go out and look for some blankets and stuff. Then we could have a meal somewhere and see what's on at the movies."

Bonny wasn't a person to remain down for very long. By the time they had purchased half a dozen cheap blankets (dirty gray with red stripes), a couple of foam-filled pillows, and a stock of candles and some little tin trays on which to stand them, she was showing definite signs of recovery. It was Bonny who decreed what they should eat (hamburgers and French fries from the local McDonald's) and Bonny who chose which movie they should see. The choice of film was somewhat limited by the fact that she only liked horror movies and there was only one theater within walking distance that was showing any.

They spent the evening watching a double bill of *Plague Monsters* and *Zombies From the Deep* in a theater with slashed seats and a faulty sound system, with things going on in the shadows that Richard hardly liked to think about. Bonny didn't seem to notice the sound system, or the goings-on. She sat engrossed, biting her nails like a child at all the most scarifying bits and during the last few minutes of *Zombies From the Deep*, even slipping her hand into Richard's and gripping it rather tightly.

He couldn't make up his mind how he felt about Bonny taking his hand. It didn't displease him, but did it actually *please* him? And if so, how did it please him? Did it please him physically, or did it just please him mentally? He was so busy trying to analyze his emotions that he very nearly missed the climax of the film, which would have been a pity since it showed all the zombies spectacularly shriveling to nothing underwater, zapped by the hero's psycho-ray gun.

"That was *good*," said Bonny as they left the theater. "I liked that. Didn't you?"

He said yes because it would have seemed intellectually snobbish to say no; and anyway, if he were to be honest he would have to admit that he had enjoyed it far more than he thought he was going to, even if he hadn't yet managed to resolve his feelings about what happened toward the end. Did Bonny always automatically hold hands in the movies? Would she hold hands with just anyone? Had she expected *him* to be the one to hold *hers*?

On the way home—now that they had a few bits and pieces he was half beginning to think of it as "home"— they stopped off at a stand selling seafood and Bonny ate some clams while Richard had a cup of tea (and with some reluctance allowed a clam to be pushed into his mouth). Bonny beamed up at him trustfully.

"This is fun," she said, "isn't it?"

She said something very similar when they got back: "It's nice in here now. Don't you think it's nice?"

It certainly wasn't as bad as it had been. They had their blankets and their pillows, with the candles burning in their little tin trays on top of the ancient gas stove and the blue-painted kitchen dresser, which Richard, in an attempt at preserving modesty, had maneuvered into the center of the room to serve as a makeshift partition.

"It *is* nice," said Bonny, "isn't it?" Her voice came to him from the other side of the gas stove.

"Yes," he said. "It's much better."

"You didn't like it yesterday, did you?"

"That's probably because I was tired."

"I knew you didn't like it." Bonny was silent a moment, then, "You're not asleep, are you?" she asked.

"No," he said, "I'm reading." He turned a page. Bonny's head suddenly appeared over the top of the gas stove.

"Are you warm enough?"

"Yes," he said. "Why? Aren't you?"

"*I* am. I just thought, if you weren't . . . I mean, if you wanted . . . if you'd like . . ." She trailed off. "It must be ever so hard," she said, "sleeping on that bottom bit."

"It's all right," he said.

"But it hasn't any springs."

"Doesn't bother me."

"Oh. Well, if you're sure—"

"Honestly," said Richard, "I'm fine."

It wasn't until later, when he blew out the candles, that he realized what she had been offering him.

9
Chapter

". . . I always knew that it would be a mistake, breaking it to them like that. You seem to imagine that everyone's the way your mother is, not caring about what people are, or what they do, just so long as it's not antisocial, but my parents aren't like that. They think there's only one way to be, and that's the way they are, and that anyone who's different has got to be wrong. And when it's something to do with sex, then they think it's not only wrong but immoral. They get very bothered by people's morals. My old man gets very vituperative about them. The things he says are the sort of things that you think people don't say anymore, but they do, and that's one of the reasons I didn't want to tell them, or at least not yet. Not because I'm secretly ashamed, which is what

you said, nor because I feel guilty, or think we're doing anything wrong. I wouldn't have minded everybody else knowing, I just didn't want them to, but you had to go and make a big production of it, make out it was a matter of principle. I told you what would happen. I said the old man would blow a gasket, and now . . ."

Richard stopped, appalled. This wasn't the letter he had meant to write. It was heaping all the blame on Jan and accepting none of it himself; and furthermore, it wasn't even truthful. Nobody had *forced* him into telling his parents. If Jan's arguments had finally proved more persuasive than his, that was because Jan had been arguing from a position of honesty and he hadn't. All along he had had his mean little doubts, his reservations, an ultimate reluctance to commit himself. He had never confessed to any of it, but Jan had known.

He looked down at the page he had written. He couldn't send that. Disgusted, he ripped it off the pad, screwed it up, and threw it into the fireplace, which they had taken to using as a wastepaper basket. It was a letter he would write later, when he had had a chance —a proper chance—to come to grips with his emotions and work out how he felt. For the moment he would stick to simpler things. The house. The room. He could tell Jan about the room, about the other tenants. He didn't have to mention Bonny. Or he could tell about his job. He had been working for Market Decisions for nearly two weeks now; he was becoming quite an old hand at picking up the telephone and entering into conversation with total strangers. He could write about that.

He glanced at his watch and saw that it was just after three o'clock. He had arranged with Bonny that at quarter past three he would go into her supermarket and stock up with all the goods they would be likely to need for the coming week. They had sat together the previous evening and made out a long list.

"Canned stuff," Bonny had said. "Like baked beans, or soup; stuff that's easy to heat up. Or sardines, or ham. Stuff like that. Stuff that doesn't need cooking. And bread and fruit and cheese, and that sort of thing, only not the blue sort of cheese 'cause I don't like the blue sort. And the only soup I like is tomato—and sardines in sauce, not oil. I don't like them in oil. And I don't like oranges, and I don't like bananas, and I don't like onions—I don't mind *pickled* onions. And condensed milk. I like condensed milk, all thick and gluggy. You could get lots of cans of that. But you've got to come in at quarter past three. *Exactly.*"

She had been very definite about him going in at quarter past three. It seemed that that was the hour when Bonny returned from her afternoon break and someone named Alice went off to have hers. He couldn't quite grasp the significance of Alice going off, except that she was a supervisor and appeared to have some kind of grudge against Bonny. She mightn't like it, Bonny had said, if she caught her serving someone she actually knew. Richard had suggested that in that case perhaps he ought to go to a different checkout, or even to a different store, but Bonny had looked at him rather fiercely and said, "No, you've got to come to *me*. Just pretend you don't know me. That's all. And remember, *quarter past three*."

If he didn't get a move on he wouldn't get there on time, and then she would be mad at him. He would have to write to Jan another day. Maybe tomorrow. Tomorrow was Sunday; he would be able to lie in bed and assemble his thoughts.

He fought his way through the crowded Saturday streets, reaching Bonny's supermarket with a minute to spare. Behind one of the registers he caught a glimpse of her, back from her break, looking smart and efficient in a green nylon smock with a little green cap perched on her head. He supposed she wouldn't mind him going in a minute early. Helping himself to a cart he set off down the first aisle with his shopping list.

By the time he arrived back at the checkout counter with a full load Bonny had a line of several people waiting. The lines on either side were shorter, but he didn't like to join them in case she felt slighted. For all her talk of hating work she evidently wanted him to see her in action. Obediently he stacked up all his cans and cartons on the moving belt and awaited his turn. When it came, Bonny said, "You'll need some of these" and thrust a couple of plastic shopping bags at him. Then she said, "Hold them open and I'll pack for you." He watched, mesmerized, a ten-pound note ready in his hand, as Bonny punched up the prices, snatched up the goods, stashed them into the bag: *punch, snatch, stash; punch, snatch, stash*—no wonder she had wanted him to see her. She was obviously highly skilled at her job.

" 'Kyou!" Briskly she whipped the ten-pound note away from him, slapped a fistful of change into his hand, shunted his bags out of the way, and turned her attention to the next customer.

A trifle dazed by the speed of it all, he moved down after his bags, putting his hand, with the change, into his jeans pocket.

Something was wrong: he shouldn't have all those one-pound pieces.

He pulled his hand back out and examined the money. He never bothered adding up the prices as he went around (Jan did, but Jan, being a computer person, had a mind like a calculating machine), but even he was capable of realizing that you couldn't purchase a whole cart of goods and still have eight pounds change from a ten-pound note. Bonny must have mistaken it for a twenty. He turned to say something.

"Excuse me, I think—"

Bonny's head whipped round. The words froze on his lips. What had happened? Had the dreaded Alice come back? He hesitated.

Bonny's face had turned bright crimson. Agonized fury flashed in her eyes. She plainly didn't realize what she had done; she just wanted him to get out before Alice should discover him. But what was Alice going to say when they checked the registers at the end of the afternoon and found that Bonny's was several pounds short? She would be furious.

Resolutely he waited, hovering by the checkout as Bonny emptied a cart full of cat food cans and tonic water and giant bags of frozen peas. Suddenly, as she leaned forward to claw up the last of the cat food tins, she turned her head sideways toward him like a swimmer doing the crawl and mouthed just two words: *Bug off!*

You didn't stay to argue with someone who mouthed *Bug off* at you; not unless you wanted to provoke a scene, which was the last thing he desired. He pushed the money back into his pocket, picked up his bags, and fled the store, expecting any moment to feel a hand upon his shoulder and the invitation to "Step this way a moment, if you wouldn't mind."

Back home in their room, putting away the cans of condensed milk and tomato soup in the blue-painted dresser, he came across the receipt. He ought to keep it, he thought, to show Bonny. The total must come to at least ten pounds, if not more.

He looked down at it: it said £1.50. For a moment he thought she must have given him the wrong one, but then he counted the number of items and they came to twenty-nine, and he counted the number of items in the dresser cupboard and they also came to twenty-nine, and he knew then that she hadn't given him the wrong one, and she hadn't mistaken his ten-pound note for a twenty. She had undercharged him quite deliberately.

He stood staring at the contents of the cupboard and felt himself turn goose-pimply and cold. For the first time in his life he had participated in a criminal act: these were stolen goods, and he was in possession of them. Any second and there could be a knock at the door and the police would be there with a search warrant and a warrant for his arrest. His old man would have an apoplexy. SON OF LOCAL BUSINESSMAN HELD ON CHARGES OF THEFT. It would just about finish his mother. Was Bonny bananas?

His first panic-stricken impulse was to bundle everything back into the two plastic shopping bags as fast as

91

he could go and drive out with them into the country, deep into the depths of some dark forest, where he could dig a hole and bury them. What stopped him was not so much the fact that he couldn't immediately think of any dark forest as fear of what Bonny would say when she arrived back to find an empty cupboard.

He decided that he would compromise by removing all the price tags from the cans and stuffing the shopping bags behind the broken toilet in the first-floor bathroom, and that when Bonny came in he would take a stern line with her. He knew that lots of people *did* steal from supermarkets, and he wouldn't want to be thought lily-livered, but Bonny didn't have a father who was a pillar of the establishment or a mother who suffered from a nervous disposition. And anyway, stealing things wasn't right, whichever way you looked at it; surely even Bonny must be capable of seeing that?

It took him the whole of the rest of the afternoon to destroy the evidence. Some of the price tags refused to come off and had to be soaked for ages in hot water, which in turn had to be boiled for ages on the gas burner in the kitchen. Then when all the tags were off he suddenly had second thoughts about the shopping bags and felt impelled to remove them from their hidey-hole behind the toilet and smuggle them down the road beneath his jacket. He had only been back a few minutes when there was the sound of furious foot-steps clattering up the stairs, the door was thrown open, and Bonny flew in.

"Are you *bonkers*?" She stood, a small bundle of rage, confronting him across the room. "You nearly went and blew it, dithering about like that!"

He nearly went and blew it? He liked her cheek!

"How was I to know what you were planning to do? If you'd told me beforehand—"

"If I'd told you beforehand you'd have gone all mealymouthed and wouldn't have done it!"

"No, I wouldn't, and neither ought you!"

"*Why not?*" She demanded it of him fiercely. "What's your game, capitalist lackey?"

He resented being called a lackey—*and* being called a capitalist, considering he hadn't a penny piece of capital.

"I haven't got any game! But you can't just go around stealing things."

"It's not stealing, it's taking back what's rightfully ours." Jake had gone to great lengths to explain it to her: "When the capitalists exploit the workers they call it making a profit, right? When the workers try exploiting the capitalists they call it theft. *I* call it getting a bit of our own back. Nothing wrong with that." Jake had come into Matheson's regularly once a week to exploit the capitalists and get a bit of his own back. She hadn't seen any reason why she and Richard shouldn't do the same. She hadn't realized he'd be quite so dumb—actually trying to *tell* someone they'd given him too much change! She might have known he'd go all moral on her.

"It's all very well for you." She slammed the door crossly behind her. "Always being so *goody-goody;* always going on about the rest of us."

"I don't go on about the rest of you!"

"Yes, you do," said Bonny. "You went on about Sheena, you went on about the noise . . ."

He hadn't gone on about Sheena. All he'd said—and that was only to Bonny—was that just because the place was a squat he didn't see why people had to throw cigarette butts all over the hall floor. As for the noise, it had been three o'clock in the morning and he hadn't *complained*, he'd just taken the pillow from Bonny's side of the partition and put it on top of his head to try to muffle the sound. When she'd arrived upstairs and asked him what he was doing, he'd told her; that was all.

"If you'd joined in," said Bonny, "you wouldn't have *noticed* the noise."

"I did join in." He had stayed with them, down in the communal kitchen, for almost two hours. Then he felt he'd had enough. He'd wanted to get away after that and be by himself to read his book.

"You don't like them," said Bonny, "do you?"

"I don't *dis*like them."

"But you don't *like* them."

It wasn't that he didn't like them so much as that they were totally outside his experience. There was Sheena, who dropped cigarette butts and was probably on drugs; John, who had just been released from prison and had nowhere else to go; Alison, who dyed her hair in a rainbow arc of colors and walked the streets barefoot—even Bonny said that Alison was "raving way out." Even so, he didn't dislike her. He didn't dislike any of them, he just didn't know how to talk to them. They seemed to speak a different language. Sometimes when he said things to them they looked at him as though he were crazy or from another planet.

"You don't like Vic," said Bonny.

"No." It was true that Vic wasn't one of his favorite people. He had the face of a Botticelli angel and little darting bright eyes like glass marbles. Richard never felt quite comfortable when Vic was around.

"You've had it in for him right from the beginning," said Bonny. "Just 'cause I went and talked to him."

"It's nothing to do with you talking to him!"

"So what is it, then?"

Richard hesitated, trying to work out to his own satisfaction what it was about Vic that he didn't like. "Well, for one thing," he said, "I don't see why he charges people rent."

"Why shouldn't he charge people rent?"

"Because it's not his house!"

"It was him that found it," said Bonny.

"Yes, but he doesn't *own* it."

"So what?"

So it wasn't right, that was what. He was surprised Bonny couldn't see it for herself. She accused him of being a capitalist lackey, then happily went and handed over half her weekly wages as blood money to Vic.

"He's got to make a living, hasn't he, the same as everyone else?"

"I don't see why he should make it out of *us.*"

"Because it was him that took all the risks, breaking in and everything. He could have got himself arrested for that."

"Yes, and you could have got arrested," said Richard, "doing what you did this afternoon."

Bonny tossed her head. "They wouldn't arrest me! I'd say it was a mistake."

"A mis*take*? On *twenty-nine items*?"

"Well, then, I'd say I'd had a blackout. I'd say ev-

95

erything had suddenly gone blank and I didn't know what I was doing. *Then* they wouldn't arrest me."

"No, they'd just fire you so you'd be out of a job!"

"So who cares?" The tears suddenly sprang to Bonny's eyes. "I'd just as soon be out of a job. I *hate* it, going in there. It's boring—it's *stupid.* Just sitting taking money, packing bags . . ." She dashed a hand across her eyes. "Might as well be *dead.*"

Richard frowned. He cleared his throat. It embarrassed him when Bonny cried, just as it embarrassed him when his mother did. "Surely" he said tentatively, not wanting to provoke a flood, "surely it can't be as bad as all that." He could understand that she mightn't want to sit behind a cash register for the rest of her life (now that the initial gloss had worn off, he knew that *he* wouldn't want to spend the rest of his life asking people which television commercials they had recently watched), but it couldn't be all unrelieved gloom.

"It's all right for you!" She flung it at him like an accusation. "You're at college!"

"So perhaps that's where you ought to be."

"Me?"

"Why not?"

Fresh tears spurted from her eyes.

" 'Cause you have to have exams!"

"Well, you could get some. You could study for them."

She hiccuped mistrustfully. "H-how?"

"All sorts of ways; evening classes, correspondence courses, OU—"

"What's OU?"

"Open university. Lots of people study through the open university." Jan's mother did. She was taking a course in philosophy at the moment. According to Jan, she was always doing a course on something or other.

"So how d'you get in there?" said Bonny. "Without 'ny exams?"

"You don't need exams. That's the whole point of it, that's why it's called *open*. Because it's for everyone."

"Even if they're stupid?"

"Well, yes, I suppose. In theory. But you're not stupid!"

"Yes, I am." The tears came afresh. She seemed, like his mother, to have a natural facility for crying. "*They* said I was. At school. They said. They wouldn't let me take things, they said I was too *stupid*."

"Well, then, they were obviously stupid! What about your favorite subject?"

"Hist'ry?" She sniffed doubtfully. "What about it?"

"Wouldn't they even let you take that?"

"Wouldn't let me take *any*thing."

Quickly, before yet another flood of tears could burst upon them, he said, "All right, if you don't believe me, I'll *prove* it to you!" He turned and snatched up one of his George Orwells; he had a stack of them by now. Since reading *Down and Out* he had gone up the road and bought a whole lot more in paperback. "This is a book called"—he looked down at it—"*Animal Farm,* written by George Orwell. He also wrote something called *1984,* which you may have heard of."

Bonny brightened. "I saw it on television; it was great."

He didn't say that he had also seen it on television and that he had thought the book was far better. He wouldn't want to discourage her before they had even begun.

"Good," he said. "Now, you sit down there"—he pointed to her mattress; meekly, Bonny sat—"and listen. I'm going to read something from *Animal Farm,* and when I've read it I'm going to ask you questions about it. Okay?" She nodded. "So I'll choose a passage at random . . ." He did so. "Are you ready? Right. Here we go."

He enjoyed reading from *Animal Farm,* and Bonny, it seemed, enjoyed listening. She did it very intently, sitting cross-legged on her mattress with her chin cupped in her hands, her eyes earnestly fixed upon his face, and afterward, when he asked his questions, answered him promptly and with every indication of having understood perfectly well what it was about.

"There you are," he said. "I told you you weren't stupid!"

Bonny beamed. "Can we do some more?" she said. "From another book?"

"All right, if you like. We'll do some from *1984.*"

After doing some from *1984* they did some from *Down and Out,* which Bonny said sounded like a good book—"Can I borrow it? I'll be ever so careful"—and after *Down and Out* they opened a selection of their illicit cans, because even Richard had to agree that it would be silly to waste them now that they *had* stolen them, and had a supper of sardines with cold sweet corn, a tin of peaches with condensed milk, and a carton of fresh apple juice.

After supper Bonny wanted to know whether *she* could try doing some reading and asking Richard questions, so she treated him to some passages from her book about the Plague and the Fire of London, which was called *Forever Amber* after the main character, who was "not exactly a whore, but sort of." The passages she read were rather lurid—he didn't think it was quite the kind of book that would be required for university entrance—but Bonny assured him with relish that "There's lots worse later on. You want to read about when they get the plague. They get covered all over in these buboes, which come up in great black foul, suppurating lumps, and when they burst they splatter this yellow gunge all over the place and stink." Richard said, "Gosh!" for want of anything more intelligent.

"Gosh!" mimicked Bonny. She giggled. "What's 'gosh' s'posed to be?"

"I don't really know." He'd never given it much thought. "I suppose it's just a sort of . . . exclamation."

"Like screw," said Bonny. "Or frig."

"Well—yes. I suppose."

She studied him reflectively, her head to one side.

"D'you mind me saying frig?"

"It's not really any of my business."

No, that was true; it wasn't. Still, if he didn't like it . . . "I won't, if you'd rather I didn't. You've only got to say. I mean, I wouldn't want to embarrass you."

"You don't embarrass me."

"I bet I do," she said. "I bet I embarrassed you this afternoon." A hint of challenge was in her voice.

"You didn't embarrass me," he said.

"I bet I did!" There was a pause. "You just don't want to admit it," said Bonny.

"Why shouldn't I want to admit it?"

" 'Cause it would embarrass you!" Bonny gave a peal of delighted laughter and fell against him on the mattress. "You'd be too embarrassed to admit you were embarrassed!"

What was embarrassing him just at this moment was the fact that Bonny was rolling about all over him.

"You're funny," she said. "D'you know that?"

He swallowed. "How am I funny?"

"Things you say."

"What things do I say?"

"Gosh! Golly! Crumbs!" Bonny sat back on her heels on the mattress. "Why d'you wear glasses?"

"Because I'm shortsighted."

"I wouldn't wear them even if I *was* shortsighted."

"You would," said Richard.

Jan was always on at him to ditch his glasses. Sometimes, as a concession, he tried walking around without them, but it was like walking in a mist: it didn't feel safe. Besides, it was very inconvenient not being able to read the names of streets or make out the numbers of buses until they were virtually on top of you.

"You ought to get contact lenses," said Bonny. "That's what I'd do. Glasses make you look all pompous." She suddenly leaned forward and twitched them off. "*That's* better! You're quite nice-looking without them."

That was what Jan had said: "You don't look half bad without them." He thought about Jan, and about the letter that tomorrow morning he was definitely going to write.

"What do *I* look like?" said Bonny.

He screwed up his eyes, peering at her in the flickering light of the candles. She had balanced his glasses on the end of her short nose and had her chin tilted toward him in an effort to keep them from slipping off. He laughed. "Ridiculous!"

"Very ridiculous?"

"Absurd."

Bonny giggled and collapsed in a heap on top of him with her head pressed into his midriff. He knew, in that moment, that if he were to make the first move Bonny would not say no.

Seconds passed, and felt like minutes. There was a trickle of sweat in the middle of his back and beads of it under his hair. Bonny raised her head and looked up at him, the glasses at a rakish angle on her nose.

"I guess I'd better have them back," said Richard. "They're the only ones I've got."

Solemnly she took them off and handed them to him. He busied himself with the edge of his sweater, wiping them clean. He was aware, as he did so, of Bonny watching him.

"Do you"—*huff* on the glass, wipe, wipe—"want to go out for a coffee?"

"Do you?" said Bonny.

"I just thought"—*huff,* wipe—"it seemed like a good idea."

Slowly, Bonny uncrossed her legs. "I suppose," she said, "we might as well."

10
Chapter

Doing telephone research for Market Decisions was a fairly free and easy sort of job. You could not only choose which days you wanted to work but also which hours, so that if one morning you happened to oversleep and didn't get in until eleven or twelve, or maybe didn't even manage to get in at all, nobody minded. Nobody put black marks against your name or threatened you with dismissal. Bonny grumbled that it didn't sound to her as if it were a job at all.

"Just because it's all students and *clever* people."

"It's not *all* students," said Richard. "There's quite a few that are actors and actresses."

Bonny ignored this. She seemed totally to have forgotten that she had told him she was an actress.

"Just walk in and out as if it were a leisure center. I

s'pose they don't even tell you when you have to go for tea and coffee?"

"Not really. It's up to you. Go when you feel like going."

"Honestly!" said Bonny.

Generally Richard tried to time it so that he was alone when he went for his. He pretended to himself that it was because he liked the opportunity to read, but he knew that that was only half true. The real reason was that he was too shy to talk to people. He didn't mind asking them questions on the telephone, because then he had a questionnaire to follow. It was when he had to think of things of his own to say that he became tongue-tied.

One morning when he was drinking his solitary coffee and reading a book he had just recently discovered, *Brave New World* by Aldous Huxley, a girl came in. He had seen her once or twice before, sitting in one of the telephoning booths in the row behind his, but they had never actually spoken. Now she slammed the door shut behind her, flounced across to the coffee machine, rammed home a coin and said, "Busybodying old crone!"

Richard paused, uncertain, in his reading. The girl snatched her coffee from the machine and flung herself down in the chair next to his.

"Gets on my flaming nerves!"

He surmised that she was talking about Miss Collins, who sometimes came down from her personnel office in order to pick up the master telephone and listen in on people's conversations.

" 'I'm only checking that you're doing it right.' For crying out loud! What can you do *wrong*? Unless you're some kind of lower-grade moron." The girl thrust back her hair. It was lint white, very long and straight, as if it had been ironed. "If I don't know the job by now—" She broke off, looking at Richard. "What are you, a student?"

"Yes."

"College?" She leaned forward to peer at his book. *Brave New World* . . . never read it. Saw a production of it once. I'm in the theater, I only do this crap in between. When I absolutely have to. At least it's better than scrubbing floors—though I don't know; I sometimes wonder, the junk they give you. I mean, asking people how much they earn, for heaven's sake! And, 'Who's head of the household?' In *this* day and age?"

"I think what they mean is, who's the chief breadwinner."

"Then why don't they say so, instead of all this head of the household stuff? Haven't they ever heard of women's lib?"

Richard fell silent. He wondered if she were what Jan called "a heavy fem." She didn't look like one. The few heavy fems they had at college tended to be rather butch and strident and full of Hate Men. This one seemed more full of Hate Miss Collins than Hate Men, and she certainly wasn't butch. She was wearing a filmy, peasant-type blouse, all see-through and off-the-shoulder, with a big billowy skirt cinched in tight at the waist with a red leather belt. He supposed she was what most people would call sexy.

The silence prolonged itself until he began to feel uncomfortable. He would have liked to go back to his book, but in the circumstances it hardly seemed very polite. "What—er—sort of work do you do in the theater?" he said.

"Acting work, when I can get it."

"I know someone who's an actress," said Richard.

"Really? What's her name?"

"Bonny McEvoy."

"Bonny McEvoy?" The girl's eyes—greeny-gray with flecks of amber—opened wide. "I know Bonny!"

"I believe she was up at Crewe," said Richard.

"That's right, that's where I met her. I was in the rep." There was a pause. The girl was looking at Richard in what could only be described as a quizzical fashion. "So Bonny told you she was an actress, did she?"

"Well . . . yes," said Richard.

"I suppose she didn't tell you that she'd trained at RADA, by any chance?"

Richard's cheeks grew slowly crimson. He had noticed before that Bonny wasn't always strictly truthful: he had known for a long time that she had never really been an actress. Why, for heaven's sake, had he had to go and drag her into it?

Because he was an idiot, that was why. Couldn't hold a normal conversation without growing desperate for something to say, so just grabbed at the first stupid thing that came to mind.

"Oh, don't worry," said the girl. "You're not the first. She once told *me* she was born and brought up in a shoe box. Something like that. You can't believe a thing she says; she's a complete fantasist. What's she up to at the moment?"

"She's working in this supermarket."

"Here in London? So where's she living?"

"We're in an empty old building."

"What, you and Bonny? Together?"

He hesitated; then he said, "Yes."

"Wow! She's come up in the world."

He didn't see how anyone could possibly be said to have come *up* in the world, living in the sort of conditions that he and Bonny were living in. It was difficult to conceive of anything very much worse.

"No, I mean—" The girl waved a hand. "Quality already!"

He wondered what she was talking about. She sipped her coffee, considering him as she did so from beneath long, sweeping lashes, spiky-thick with mascara. He was glad that Bonny didn't wear mascara. Come to think of it, Bonny didn't wear any makeup at all. She didn't need to.

"The guy she used to shack up with . . . Jake. He was something else. Has she told you about Jake?"

He shook his head.

"Oh! My mistake. Perhaps I shouldn't have mentioned him. I just thought, knowing Bonny, . . . I'd have thought by now you'd have had the full rundown. Like how he was some kind of a cross between royalty and Michael Jackson."

Richard looked at her, amazed. "Is he?"

"You must be joking! More like a cross between Bugsy Malone and a gorilla. Real rough trade. All right if you happen to fancy a bit of butch, but not exactly the stuff a nice girl's dreams are made of. That's why I said quality already!"

Richard frowned, not quite sure even now that he fully understood what she was referring to. She finished her coffee and crumpled the plastic cup, lobbing

106

it accurately across the room into the wastepaper basket.

"I wouldn't mind seeing Bonny again. Why don't I come around sometime?"

"Yes," he said. "Why not?"

"How about this evening? Will you be in?"

"Er—yes," he said. "As far as I know."

"So what's the address?"

He gave it to her. "You have to come in through the back; the front's all boarded up."

"I'll find it. By the way, the name's Elaine. Just tell Bonny, Elaine from Crewe. She'll remember."

That evening, when Bonny arrived back from work, he said, "I met a friend of yours today. Someone who knew you up in Crewe."

"Oh?" She looked up at him quickly. Jake?

"Someone named Elaine."

Elaine. "That cow!"

"She said she'd like to see you again."

"Well, I don't want to see *her* again!"

"Oh." That rather nonplussed him. Now what was he supposed to do?

Bonny looked at him accusingly. "You haven't gone and asked her around here?"

"She wanted to know if she could come. This evening—"

"This *evening*?"

"Well, yes."

"And you went and told her she could?"

"I didn't see how I could very well say anything else. She gave the impression she was a friend of yours."

"She's not a friend of mine; I can't stand her. She's a *cow*. I s'pose you fancy her?"

"No." He could honestly say that he did not.

Bonny regarded him through narrowed eyes. She plainly didn't believe him. "So what's she want to come around here for?"

"I told you, she wants to see you."

"What for?" She and Elaine had never been friends; Jake had been their only point of contact. Perhaps she wanted to find out from Bonny whether Jake was still up in Crewe. Well, if that were the case she would be unlucky, because Jake was in Ireland doing his singing. Noisily she wrenched open the door of the kitchen dresser and clattered about among the cans.

"I'm going downstairs when I've had supper. If she wants to see me she can come down there. If not, she can stay up here with you. But *I'm* not staying up here."

The thought of being left alone with Elaine panicked him. She was the sort of girl who tied his tongue into knots.

"She'll have to come in through the back way," he said, "so if you were to keep an eye open for her—"

"*I'm* not keeping an eye open!" Bonny tossed her head. "Why should I? You were the one that invited her."

"Yes, but you're the one she's coming to see."

"If you believe that," said Bonny, "you'd believe anything. It's you she's after. Man-mad, she is. Far as I'm concerned, you're welcome to her. Whatever turns you on."

"But she doesn't turn me on!"

"Oh, go pull the other one!" said Bonny.

108

Who did he think he was kidding? Crossly she sawed the corner off a milk carton (milk, predictably, went spurting over the floor). That cow had run circles around Jake; now she was going to run them around Richard as well. Bonny wasn't good enough for him: she wasn't classy enough. She'd stopped swearing (almost) and she'd stopped stealing, but she still wasn't classy enough. Just like Jake hadn't been classy. She and Jake were two of a kind.

Down in the kitchen after supper she found Vic and Sheena. Sheena wanted to know what had happened to "your boyfriend."

"He's not my boyfriend." You couldn't call someone a boyfriend who slept in the same room with you and never so much as looked at you. He hadn't even held her hand when they'd gone to the movies.

"Well, whatever he is." Sheena threw her cigarette butt onto the floor and ground it in with the heel of her shoe. "What's he up to?"

"I dunno. Reading, I expect."

"Bit of a weirdo, in't he?"

"Bleedin' bananas, if you ask me." Vic swung his feet up onto the kitchen table. "Right fruit and nut case."

"He's an intellectual," said Bonny.

"What I said: bleedin' bananas."

At a quarter to eight John arrived to cook his supper on the gas burner, and shortly afterward Alison drifted in, barefoot as usual, complaining about broken glass on the sidewalk.

"Well, what d'you expect," said Vic, "walking round like that?"

"Don't expect glass," said Alison, "do you? Not on a pavement."

"I do," said Vic.

"Yeah, well, you would. You're probably the one that put it there. Cut me foot on that lot, I could go septic."

"That's what buboes go," said Bonny, "in this book I'm reading. This one about the Plague and the—"

Loud groans from Vic and Alison.

"Not *that* again," said Sheena.

Affronted, Bonny turned away to talk to John. She was still talking to him minutes later when she became aware of the kitchen door opening and a new presence entering the room. Determinedly, she kept her back turned.

"Bonnee!" Elaine's voice came floating over, all high-pitched and tinkling. Bell-like, they had called it when she played Portia in *The Merchant of Venice.* Squeaky was the way it sounded to Bonny. "How *are* you?"

Bonny turned reluctantly. "All right."

"Imagine finding you in London! I couldn't believe it when Richard said Bonny McEvoy!" Over Elaine's shoulder, Richard directed an agonized glance toward Bonny. "Bonny *McEvoy*? I said. *Jake's* Bonny? Bonny from Crewe? Down *here*? And there's me and Richard working all the time in the same place and never realizing. Talk about coincidence!"

"It's a small world," said Vic.

"Isn't it just?" Elaine shot Bonny a mischievous smile. "Especially in the theater."

Vic pounced eagerly. "Oh! You're in the theater, are you? I once thought of going into that field—not as an

110

actor, of course. More an impresario sort of thing; pro-
ducer, like. Lot of money to be made in producing.
Just got to make sure you choose the right
show. . . ."

Richard was making urgent faces at Bonny across
the room. She went over to him. "What's the matter?"

"Shall I go up to the pub and get a bottle?"

"What for?"

He gestured. "She brought one."

"So what do we want another for?"

"Well . . . I don't know." He shrugged a shoulder.
"I just thought perhaps I ought."

"Don't see why you should go buying bottles. Just
come and sit down"—she tugged at him—"and stop
fussing."

Stop fussing; stop agitating. She sounded like Jan.
Resigned, Richard allowed himself to be towed across
the room.

"Wasn't even as if she was invited: invited herself. *I*
didn't want to see the woman." Bonny sat down with
an aggressive plonk on the block of foam rubber that
served as a couch. "Stupid cow."

John made coffee one cup at a time on the gas heater
and dished it out in relays; Elaine's bottle circulated,
going from hand to hand. There weren't any glasses for
the wine and only three cups for the coffee, so Richard
and Bonny shared one between them, taking alternate
sips.

"Who's the bird?" John wanted to know. "Friend of
yours?"

"Not so's you'd notice," said Bonny.

"So what's she doing here?"

"Don't ask me. He's the one that asked her."

"I didn't ask her! She said she wanted to see you. How was I to—"

"Oh, stop keeping on!" said Bonny. She saw Elaine glance in their direction. "Here!" She put the coffee cup to Richard's lips. "Have another sip."

Elaine needn't think that just because she was no longer with Jake she hadn't got anyone. She wriggled up closer to Richard on the foam rubber block. He mightn't be as exciting as Jake, but he was really far nicer. *Far* nicer. Richard wasn't the sort to ever walk out on anyone. And he never made horrid remarks, or said things to hurt. It was a pity, perhaps, that he couldn't be a bit more . . . well, just a bit more . . .

"Old Vic's trying his luck," said John.

Men always did with Elaine. She supposed, really, that that was the thing that made Richard so nice: he wasn't like most men. *He* didn't keep wanting to maul you all the time, or get you into bed. You could snuggle up to him, as she did now—

"We've run out of booze!"

That was Vic, disgusting pig. Vic *was* disgusting. She'd gone right off him after seeing him tonight, smarming over Elaine. And anyway, Richard was right: why *should* he take rent off people? It wasn't his property. Wasn't as if he'd done anything, other than smash a window to get in. Anyone could just do that. Didn't take any special talent.

"We're out of booze! Who's going to go down the pub?"

"I'll go," said Richard.

Bonny snatched indignantly at his sleeve. "Why you?"

"It's all right. I won't be long."

112

"But it shouldn't *be* you!"

Why should he be the one to fork out? It ought to be Vic, if anybody. He was the one that had been doing all the smarming, not to mention most of the drinking. Richard was too easy, that was his trouble. If that had been Jake—

If that had been Jake, Jake would have been the one doing all the smarming. It was *loath*some the way he'd fawned on Elaine.

Across the room Vic was playing the big wheel, trying to impress, telling Elaine all about how he'd found this empty house and decided to take it over. How he was seriously thinking of going into business as Victor Properties Limited.

"Got to be limited. That way, see, if you go bust, they can't get you. Can't hold you liable. Oh, I've looked into it all, don't you worry."

Elaine was listening with her head on one side, making lots of polite little twittery noises, just as she used to do with Jake when he tried to impress.

"Bet *she* wouldn't say no," said John.

She'd said no to Jake—or had she? Bonny could never be absolutely certain. Sometimes she had her doubts, even now.

Elaine's voice came fluting over. "Talking about rooms, you ought to see some of the ones that *I*'ve had in my time. I've just come back from this tour of Ireland, and honestly . . ."

Ireland? Bonny spun around. So *that* was why Jake . . .

"Absolutely unbelievable," said Elaine. She caught sight of Bonny. "Your dump in Factory Lane was a positive palace in comparison. I saw Jake when I was

there, by the way. He came to the show a few times—
on complimentaries, needless to say! He was dead
broke as usual. He came back on the ferry with us. Not
quite what you'd call his normal sparkling self. Can
you imagine Jake being seasick? All over his guitar?
Not a pretty sight! The last I saw of him he was trying
to hitch a lift back to Crewe."

Bonny froze.

"Anyway," said Vic, "like I was telling you—"

"*Jake?*" said Bonny. "Gone back to Crewe?"

"That's where he said he was going." Elaine
laughed. "He actually wanted to come to London with
me, but I managed to knock *that* idea on the head. He
was a bit down, poor lamb. I don't think the trip to
Ireland proved quite as—*successful* as he'd hoped. If
you know what I mean."

". . . build up this empire," Vic was droning on.

Jake back in England? Jake back in *Crewe*?

"Start with hovels, move on to studios. Gradually
diversify. That's how they do it, these big tycoons."

Bonny stood, heart hammering. If she were to leave
now, *now,* this very instant, just pack her bags and
go—

Go how? By train?

There might not be one. Not this time of night. And
even if there were, she didn't have the money.

Hitch a lift?

No. She'd got away with that once, she mightn't be
so lucky a second time. Besides, it would be silly to
forfeit a week's wages. She'd only got to hang on till
tomorrow and she could go up by train *and* have something over to give Jake. If he were dead broke, he
wouldn't be very happy to see her turn up empty-

114

handed. If she waited till she'd been paid they could go out for a Chinese meal and Jake could have a glass of beer. She wouldn't have to mention about seeing Elaine; she could pretend she'd just been down to Southampton to visit Nobby and Bo and that she had never really meant to stay away permanently—which she wouldn't have, had she known he was going to come back. She wouldn't have gone away at all if she'd known that.

"The dear boy seemed to imagine," said Elaine, "that you were still going to be up there, just twiddling your thumbs and awaiting his lordship's pleasure."

"Men do," said Alison. "They're all pigs and self-opinionized."

"Lesbian cow," said Vic.

Alison turned on him.

"Yes, and you can shut it, Victor Hodgkiss! You're no better than you ought to be. If the law knew half the things that you got up to—"

"Yeah, well, they don't, so who's gonna tell them?"

"I will, if you don't wash your mouth out!"

"Children, children," said Elaine. "Let us not fall out."

"They're pigs," said Alison. "All of 'em."

Elaine tilted her head to one side. "Even Richard?"

"Richard ain't her boyfriend, and anyway he's a bleedin' nut case."

"I think he's rather sweet," said Elaine.

Sweet. It was enough to make you throw up. At least nobody could accuse Jake of being sweet. No, and nobody could accuse Bonny of it, either. She and Jake were two of a kind. Elaine could have Richard if she wanted: Bonny was going back where she belonged.

115

Friday

Dear Richard,

I will be gone by the time you get this note, I hope you will not mind but I have taken some of the cans. There are enough left for your supper. I got board doing what I was doing so have decided to go back to Crewe. I have left you my blankets and pilow. I hope you get your medeival history exams allright and can think of something interesting to do. Thank you very much for giving me a lift that day. It has been very nice meeting you and being in London. I hope that you are happy.

Love from Bonny.

She left it by the side of his bed, on top of his George Orwells, where he couldn't miss it. At least it was a nicer note than the one Jake had left her.

11
Chapter

"Stupid cow!" Jake said it, for Jake, quite good-humoredly. He reached across to help himself to some more fried rice. "Course I was gonna come back. What d'you think? I was planning to take up permanent residence? Great daft loon!"

Bonny beamed. She liked it when Jake called her a great daft loon. He only called her that when he was feeling pleased with her.

"I was right choked, I can tell you, when I got back and found you weren't there."

"But you must've known," said Bonny, "that I'd be coming back."

"Why? All I knew was what the others told me: you'd just packed your bags and gone. I'm the one that has the grievance, if anyone does."

She didn't want to start talking about grievances; not tonight. She pushed Jake's glass toward him. "You're not drinking your beer."

"I'm saving it."

"But you can have more!"

"Yeah . . . thing is, I owe Donovan. I've been bumming off him the last few days. I was totally out of funds, see, when I got back. I thought you'd be here." He looked at her across the table. "How d'you manage to get the bread if you've not been working?"

"Nobby and Bo gave it me," she lied blithely.

"Oh. Well, in that case . . . cheers!" Jake raised his beer glass. "Here's to Nobby and Bo." He finished drinking and wiped a mustache of froth off his mouth. "How are the old dykes? Still flourishing? Obviously not transferred their affections yet."

Bonny stared down, rather hard, at her plate. She wished Jake wouldn't say things like that.

"All right, all right. I was only joking! No need to get your panties in a twist." Jake leaned forward and tweaked at a lock of her hair. "*You.* Are you listening? I said, no need to get your panties in a twist. *I* haven't got anything against dykes. I was only trying to show a polite interest, find out how they are."

"They're fine," said Bonny.

"Good."

Jake munched on his crispy noodles. Bonny stabbed with her fork at a bunch of bean shoots.

"I saw Elaine when I was there."

"Elaine?" Jake looked up sharply. A piece of crispy noodle shot out of his mouth.

"In Southampton."

"Elaine?"

118

"Yes." She'd never intended bringing Elaine into it. She didn't really know why she had. Perhaps it was to pay Jake back for referring to Nobby and Bo as a couple of old dykes.

"What was she doing in Southampton?"

"Acting. I saw her at the theater. . . . She said you'd been to see her when you were in Ireland."

Jake scowled. "So?"

"So I just mentioned it," said Bonny.

"She told me she was going to London. She said she'd got a flat there."

Bonny shrugged. She couldn't help what the cow had told him. Jake studied her a moment, eyes narrowed.

"You sure it was Southampton?"

"Course I'm sure."

"So what was she acting in?"

"I dunno. Can't remember."

"That's because you're lying!"

"I'm not lying! What would I want to lie for?"

"Because you always lie, about everything. It's become second nature. You don't even have to have any reason for it anymore; you do it just for the sake of it. That's madness, that is." Jake pointed at her with his fork across the dish of fried rice. "Bananas time. You wanna watch it. You can get put away for that sort of thing."

Bonny frowned. She prodded fretfully at the congealing mess of Chinese food on her plate. She *hadn't* lied to him—well, not really. What did it matter whether she'd seen Elaine in London or in Southampton? She'd seen her, that was the point. There wasn't any need to get mad.

119

It was all going wrong. She'd only been back a few hours and here they were quarreling already. It had been lunchtime when she suddenly decided to make a break for it. She'd been paid, so why wait any longer? She'd thought Jake would be pleased. She'd thought he'd be glad to see her—especially with a week's wages and a bag full of provisions—and so he had been, just at first. It seemed it didn't take long for her to get on his nerves.

She wondered what Richard was doing. He would have got in from work by now and found her note. She hoped he wouldn't mind her making off with the cans. She'd felt bad about that afterward, when it was too late to do anything about it, though she'd left him some baked beans and a tin of pears so that he would have enough for supper.

Last Friday, she remembered, he had taken her out for a meal. Now it was her taking Jake—except that it didn't feel as if she were the one who was doing the taking, because she wasn't the one who had the money anymore. Before they came out Jake had said, "So what bread do we have?" and she had handed it all over to him. She didn't mind Jake having the money. It only seemed right that he should. He had grown a beard while he was away and let his hair grow long, so that he looked all wild and unkempt and gorgeous. She didn't see how Elaine could resist him, though she was very glad she had, since it meant that Jake had come back. She knew, in spite of what he said, that he wouldn't have done so if he could have made it with Elaine. He would be there with her now, down in London, living with her in her flat. Imagine if he had been there when Richard had met Elaine, at that place where they had worked. Imagine if—

"Hey!" Jake was snapping his fingers under her nose. "Where've you gone?"

She shook herself. "Haven't gone anywhere."

"Well, just make sure you don't. You're back with me now, right?"

Bonny nodded. "Right." She was back with Jake, where she belonged, and it was as if the last few weeks had never been.

"I suppose it was just a bit sudden," said Richard, "that's all."

"Here today, gone tomorrow; that's Bonny for you." Elaine handed him a plastic cup of coffee from the machine. "Black with no sugar, okay?"

"Yes. Thank you." If she had only said something the previous night, discussed it with him, told him what she had in mind. It would at least have prepared him. It had been a shock coming home on the Friday evening to find that she had gone; the weekend, without her, had been quite miserable. He had felt more alone during those two days without Bonny than he had on that first morning, waking up in the car, before he had met her.

"Actually," said Elaine, "I must admit, I was a bit surprised when you told me that you and she were having a thing together."

He had never told her that he and Bonny were having a thing together. She had jumped to her own conclusions. He wondered what she would say if he were to tell her now that he had never laid so much as a finger on Bonny, that he had never even kissed her.

"I mean, I know she's quite prettyish, in a street-urchin sort of way, but I just couldn't see—I mean, apart from the obvious—I just couldn't see what you'd *do* together, never mind *talk* about."

He and Bonny had talked about all kinds of things. Medieval history, George Orwell, *Forever Amber*. Except for just at first, he'd never been tongue-tied with Bonny. Like Jan, she had refused to let him.

"When it comes down to it," said Elaine, "Jake is far more her type."

Richard frowned. "I thought you said that Jake was rough trade."

"Yes. Well . . ." Elaine shrugged delicately.

He hoped she wasn't implying that Bonny was rough trade. Bonny might sometimes do things that embarrassed him, like swearing at cabdrivers or stealing from supermarkets, but there wasn't anything basically bad about her. He would hate to think of her going back to some loudmouthed bully who abused her.

"Oh, Jake wouldn't *abuse* anyone," said Elaine. "Not physically. He's not into violence. He just has this king-size chip on his shoulder."

And took it out on Bonny?

"Well, if people will grovel at his feet like some kind of doormat, what can you expect? They're bound to get themselves trampled on."

He didn't like the thought of Bonny being trampled on; she deserved better than that.

"I'm ever so sorry," said Elaine. "Really I am. It's all my fault. I ought to have kept my big mouth shut, I just never thought—I mean, running back to a clod like *Jake*." She laid a hand on Richard's arm. "Why don't you come around to our place tonight and let me cook you a meal? There's only me and a girlfriend, and she goes off to the theater at six thirty. Why don't you come?"

He swallowed. "That's v-very n-nice of you," he said. "I'd l-love to, but I've—g-got things to do. I've g-got to—"

"Wash your hair?" said Elaine.

"W-wash my hair? No, I—"

"That was a joke," she said.

"Oh. S-sorry, I—"

"*You* don't have to be sorry," said Elaine. There was a pause. She squeezed his arm. "Later in the week, perhaps?"

"Yes," he said gratefully. "That would be lovely."

"Open university?" Jake peered derisively over Bonny's shoulder. "Are you out of your tree?"

"I'm applying for details." That was what it said on the printed form she had found in the newspaper: *For details, apply to . . .* "There's no harm in just writing."

"You must be crazy! They'd never let you in there."

"Why not?"

"Because," said Jake, tapping the side of his head with a finger, "you need brains, that's why not."

"No, you don't." Richard had told her so, and Richard knew more about such matters than Jake. "Anyone can go there."

"Not if they're a flaming half-wit, they can't!"

"Shouldn't think anyone that was a flaming half-wit'd want to."

"So why do you?"

123

" 'Cause I want to get somewhere in life. I don't want to be stuck sitting behind a checkout for the rest of my days, do I?"

"Oh, oh! Aren't we getting grand? Aren't we getting ideas *au dessus de notre gare?*"

Bonny looked at him.

"I suppose we don't know what that means, do we?" said Jake. "We want to go and study at the big university and get ourselves a degree, but we can't even understand a simple little bit of Frog talk."

She tossed her head defiantly. "Could if I'd learned it. I'm not *stupid.*"

"Then why d'you act like it?"

"I don't act like it! You try reading me something, like out of a book or something, then ask me questions. Go on!"

"All right," said Jake. "Since you insist." He turned and clawed up a paper he had been reading. "This is a little article entitled 'Legalized Robbery.' Ready?"

Bonny nodded.

"Okay, then, here we go. 'The capitalist minority, that is the one percent of the population that owns more of the country's wealth than the poorer eighty percent put together, and whose power to legally rob the propertyless majority is dependent on the subservience of the latter . . .' "

Jake read for almost ten minutes. When he came to the end he said, "Well, that was simple enough. Now you give me a précis of it."

Bonny's face grew slowly pink.

"Go on, then!" said Jake. "I'm waiting."

"I didn't mean that sort of thing, I meant, read out of a *book.*"

124

"You meant read some load of crap that you could understand." Jake, disgusted, slung the paper onto the unmade bed. *"Forever* flaming *Amber*—load of drivel! You know your trouble, don't you? You've got a mind like a TV soap opera. Do they have degrees in that? If they do, you should be all right. I reckon you could get an MA in drivel. If not, you might as well forget it, 'cause you're just wasting your time. Until you've learned to master words of more than one syllable . . ."

Why did Jake always have to make out that she was stupid? She might not be clever, but she wasn't *stupid.* Richard had proved to her that she wasn't. When he had read things, she'd had no trouble at all understanding them, and Richard had read George Orwell, which not even Jake could call drivel.

"I s'pose you're just jealous," she said.

"Me? Jealous? What have I got to be jealous of?"

"Not going to college."

"I could have gone to college if I'd wanted! I chose not to. Some of us prefer to do our thinking for ourselves—those of us that *can* think." Jake flung himself moodily into the room's one and only armchair, hoisting his legs up over the side. "You'd do better going out and earning us some bread, instead of indulging yourself in fantasy time."

"Why me?" said Bonny. She felt suddenly resentful. Richard had gone out and got himself a job. *He* hadn't expected her to go out and earn for both of them. "Why not you as well?"

Jake raised an eyebrow. "Getting a bit above ourselves, aren't we? I've told you already, I don't believe in it."

"Don't believe in *what*? Earning money?"

"Working for other people, you stupid cow!"

"So why do I have to?"

"Because it doesn't bother you like it does me! With me it's a matter of principle. You wouldn't know a principle if you saw one. And anyway, you can get work in a food store; at least you get something out of it. It's about time the cupboards were stocked up again."

"I'm not doing that anymore," said Bonny.

"Not doing what anymore?"

"Stealing things."

"For crying out loud!" Jake swung his legs back to the floor with an angry thump. "How many more times do I have to tell you? It's not stealing, it's taking back what's rightfully ours. It was all there, in that piece I just read you. *Legalized robbery.* They're exploiting us right, left, and flaming center and she sits there and says, 'I'm not going to do it anymore'!"

"Well, I'm not," said Bonny.

There was a pause. "Might one inquire," Jake said in tones of honeyed sarcasm, "as to one's motives? Or would that be placing too heavy a demand upon one's intellect?"

Bonny pursed her lips. "I'm not going to do it 'cause I don't think it's right."

" 'I'm not going to do it 'cause I don't think it's right'! And you think it's right we should be *exploited*?"

"N-no, but—"

"But what?"

"But I don't see how it's going to change anything."

That was what Richard had said when they had talked

126

about it. He had agreed that things weren't what they should be, what with nuclear weapons and people starving and all the rest, but he just couldn't see how Bonny stealing things from supermarkets was going to make the situation any better. When Bonny had suggested that it would at least make *her* situation better, he had said, "But isn't that rather a narrow way of looking at things?"

"Listen, you cretin!" Jake shot out a finger, pointing it accusingly at her. "It's each man for himself, right? That's what capitalism's all about, right?"

"Right." Bonny nodded. Even Richard had agreed on that.

"So why the hell should we worry whether we're *changing* anything? You just do the best you can for yourself and let the rest of 'em go hang!"

Bonny wrinkled her brow. "But isn't that rather a narrow way of looking at things?" she asked.

"What d'you mean, narrow? What are you going on about?" Jake glared at her, suddenly suspicious. "Who's been putting all this wishy-washy mush into your head? It's that smart-mouthed git, isn't it? It's him that's been doing it to you!"

Going through her belongings one day, Jake had come across *Down and Out,* which unthinkingly—well, *half* unthinkingly—she had brought up to Crewe with her. Inside the front cover, Richard had written his name. Jake had pounced on it instantly.

"Richard Islip? Who's Richard Islip?"

She could have said that he was a friend of Nobby and Bo's. Alternatively, she could have said that the book was secondhand, or that she had found it on the train. She could have said almost anything. Instead,

127

some demon had led her to say, "If you must know, he's someone who gave me a lift. He was nice, and we talked, and he said I could have his George Orwell to read." At intervals ever since Jake had kept coming back to the subject.

"So tell me more about him, this *someone* who gave you a lift. How old was he? Where did he come from? What did he do?"

There were moments when Bonny almost wished she had never said anything. At other times she was glad she had, because it made her feel good. Jake might think she was rubbish, but Richard hadn't. He wouldn't have stayed with her if he'd thought she was rubbish.

"Filthy class traitor! Communing with the enemy."

"He wasn't an enemy," said Bonny. "He was *nice*."

"Nice!" Jake repeated the word with heavy scorn. "What's that supposed to mean? Clean-living and said his prayers every night?"

"Well, what if he did?"

"Oh, drop dead!" said Jake.

"I take it," said Elaine, "that you and Bonny *did . . .*" She paused. "I mean, you did—"

"No," said Richard.

"*No?*" said Elaine. She widened her eyes, which was a habit she had, and stared at him in wonderment. If he and Bonny *hadn't,* then what on earth had they done?

He thought back to the short time they had been together. It seemed to him that they had done all kinds of things—gone to the movies, read books, opened cans, eaten meals, discussed world affairs, argued

128

about politics, bought bits and pieces for the room. Nothing very exciting, perhaps, but he didn't remember ever having been bored.

"Well!" said Elaine. "You do amaze me."

Yes; just as he had amazed his old man. Not that *amazed* was really the right word. *Disgusted* would be more appropriate. *If you choose to conduct yourself like some diseased creature that's crawled out of a sewer* . . . He wondered if he would ever see his father again. It seemed impossible that he shouldn't, yet equally impossible that he should. He would see his mother. Surely he would see her. His crime couldn't have been so hideous and unspeakable that even she would cut him off. Or could it? Perhaps what he had done, what he had been guilty of—

He became aware that Elaine had laid her hand on his arm. Just recently she was always touching him. He had quite grown to like it with Bonny, but Elaine made him feel uncomfortable. She seemed somehow more threatening than Bonny.

"How about coming around for that meal that you didn't come for last week? Tomorrow night. How about it?"

He had a genuine excuse this time: "I'm afraid I won't be here tomorrow evening. This is my last day."

Term started next week; the apartment would be available again at the end of the week. Whether he would still be sharing with Jan . . .

"Have you got someone?" said Elaine. "At college?"

Had he? He didn't know anymore. He had never written that letter. Twice he had tried after Bonny left, and twice he had given up because he hadn't yet reached that final decision that he had to reach. It

129

wasn't a decision that Jan or anyone else could reach for him. It had to be his, and his alone.

"Someone special?" said Elaine.

He made a mumbling sound; inarticulate, noncommittal.

"Someone you're in love with?"

Why for heaven's sake couldn't he just say it? Yes— *yes!* Someone I'm in love with! And to hell with the rest of the world.

Because even now he was still too much of a coward to stand up and be counted.

"I see!" said Jake. "I see! So you actually lived with the guy?"

"Yes," said Bonny. "I actually *lived* with the guy."

"For four whole flaming weeks?"

"Yes."

"So now it comes out," said Jake. "So now we're getting to it." He took rather a deep breath. "You actually lived with him."

"Yes. I *told* you."

"You told me you were staying with the old dykes!"

"I was going to, but they weren't there. Didn't have anywhere else, did I? I had to go *some*where."

"You didn't have to go and fraternize with the enemy!"

"He's not the enemy, that's a *stupid* thing to say, you're just—"

"Ah, shuddup!" said Jake. "Where had the old dykes gone? I thought you said they never went anywhere?"

"People move, don't they? They change houses. They don't always stay in the same place."

"Oh! So they've done a bunk, have they? Skipped out and not told you? I said they'd crap all over you, their sort always do. You're so flaming gullible—"

"I'm not flaming gullible! And they haven't done a bunk, they've moved to this big house in the country and when it's ready and they're properly settled in I'm going to go there and visit them, and I can *live* there if I want, and it's got a thousand acres and I'm going to have a pony and learn to ride and—"

"Liar!" said Jake.

"It's true! I am!"

"Oh yeah? And I suppose they're going to stick a crown on your head and call you Princess Diana? Talk about a flaming psychopath! You ought to be locked up."

Bonny snatched a saucepan from the kitchen stove.

"If you say that again I'll kill you!"

"Oh, don't be so wet!" Jake wrenched the pan away from her and flung it contemptuously to the floor. "So the old dykes did a bunk and you were left high and dry, so all right! So you went and shacked up with Smarty Pants for a few weeks. So that's okay by me. We don't own each other. You do your thing, I'll do mine. But just *don't lie to me!*"

Bonny set her jaw mutinously. Jake had lied to her; why shouldn't she lie to him? He'd never told her the truth about Elaine. She had at least told him the truth about Richard.

"I suppose," Jake said abruptly, "he made out with you."

"*No.*"

"Are you lying again?" said Jake.

"No, I'm not!"

131

"So what was the matter with him?"

"Nothing was the matter with him! He was just *nice.*"

"Don't give me that crap! Nobody's that nice. He must have been a pouf."

"He was not!"

"So why didn't he make it with you?"

"Because he respected me."

Jake threw back his head and laughed. "Respected you! He was a faggot."

"He was not a faggot!"

"Course he was. Sticks out a mile. Anyway, how d'you know? You've never met any."

"I have! I've met lots! You're just trying to besmirch him."

Jake jeered. "Besmirch! Where d'you get that from? That poxy driveling book, I suppose."

Forever Amber wasn't a poxy driveling book. Richard had said that it sounded extremely interesting. He'd said if he hadn't had so many George Orwells to catch up on, he'd have liked to read it for himself. And *he* was at college.

She made the mistake of saying so to Jake. "Richard didn't think it was drivel, and *he* was at college."

"Oh, he's the cat's flaming whiskers! Eighth wonder of the flaming world! Flaming Einstein and Gandhi and Errol flaming Flynn all rolled into flaming one! If he's as flaming wonderful as you make him out to be it's no flaming wonder he didn't want you!"

"What do you mean?" said Bonny.

"Well, he wouldn't, would he? If he's so flaming perfect!"

"Why wouldn't he?"

132

" 'Cause you're a slut," said Jake.

The tears sprang to her eyes. "I'm not!"

"Course you are! Wouldn't be here with me if you weren't, would you?"

"I wish I wasn't here with you! You're horrible!"

"So if I'm so horrible, why'd you come back?"

"I don't know! I wish I hadn't!"

"I'll tell you why you came back," said Jake. "It's because you can't manage on your own. Because you're a parasite, because you cling. You're like a great tentacle. I suppose Wonderboy got sick of you and threw you out and you flew into a panic and thought, Where can I go? Who can I latch on to?"

"I didn't—and he didn't get sick of me! He was *nice!*"

"So if he was so flaming nice," said Jake, "why don't you flaming well go back to him?"

"Just for that," sobbed Bonny, "I will!"

12
Chapter

It was early afternoon when Bonny got off the bus that had brought her to Cheltenham. Her first thought had been to go back down to London, but she wasn't sure that Richard would still be there. The people at the local college of education in Crewe had already started back for their new term. She *wasn't* stupid, whatever Jake might say.

The only trouble was, she didn't know which college Richard was at. She couldn't remember him ever telling her. In fact, when she stopped to think about it, she couldn't remember him ever telling her very much about himself at all. She knew that he had a sister named Kate, who was the same age as herself, and another sister named Sue, who was married and living in the Lake District, and she knew that his parents' home was in Cheltenham. She didn't know what their address was. She had decided that she would look up the name Islip in the telephone directory and that if there were lots of them she would just have to call them all in turn until she found the right one. She was hoping that there wouldn't be; after all, Islip wasn't like Smith or Jones.

There was a telephone booth only a few yards away from where she got off the bus. All the telephone booths in the Factory Lane area had been more or less permanently vandalized. Either the glass would be smashed or the telephones ripped out; sometimes people threw up in them. This one didn't even seem to have any graffiti scribbled on the walls. Furthermore, it had its own telephone directory, complete and unmutilated, lying on a shelf. Bonny began to think that Cheltenham must be a rather respectable sort of place. She took out the directory and thumbed through the pages until she came to *I*.

Isitt, Isles, Islam . . . *Islip:* ISLIP, P.J., West Hill Court, West Hill.

It had to be the right one; there weren't any others. She stood awhile, wondering whether to call or to go there in person. It would obviously be more sensible to telephone because, after all, it could be miles away, and even when she got there there might be no one at home. On the other hand, there might be. Richard's mother might be there; she was very curious about Richard's mother. She decided to take a chance and drop by in person.

At a store a little farther on she bought a bar of chocolate to stave off stomach rumblings and asked the man behind the counter how to get to West Hill.

"West Hill?" He dropped his spectacles to the end of his nose and surveyed her doubtfully over the rims. "Got transport, have you? Or is it Shanks's pony?"

Shanks's pony? What was he talking about? "I'm walking," said Bonny.

"Not to West Hill, you're not! Get a cab, that's your best bet."

She couldn't afford a cab. The only money she had was what she had taken back from Jake—Jake was going to be furious when he found out; that was something he *would* call stealing—and the bus fare from Crewe had already made inroads into that. She had to keep the rest for finding Richard.

"Isn't there a bus?" she said.

"Get a bus if you want. Have to trek a bit on the other end."

She had to trek what seemed like a mile or two before she even reached the bus stop. Forty minutes later she was deposited in the middle of nowhere, near a signpost that told her that Titsey was one way and Ellscombe the other. The bus driver had told her to "Take the Titsey road, keep going about a couple of hundred yards, and you'll find West Hill off on your left."

The Titsey road was narrow and twisty, with no pavements, just strips of grass bounded by ditches and hedges, and fields full of cows on the other side. West Hill, when she came to it, was just as narrow and just as twisty, with the same ditches and hedges, but instead of fields full of cows there were woody areas. Every now and again she would pass a sign saying KERCHESTER'S or FIVE OAKS or BELLMAN'S, and there

136

would be gates, and a driveway leading to someone's house.

She was nearly at the top of the hill before she came to a sign saying WEST HILL COURT. There weren't any gates, simply a long, gravelly path, dark and dampish, between two rows of shiny green laurel bushes. About halfway up the laurel bushes gave way on one side to a flinty sort of wall all covered in ivy. Over the wall, in the distance, could be seen a house. It was huge and white, with dozens of windows all glinting in the sun. Bonny wondered who lived there. An earl, perhaps, or a duke. Or maybe a cabinet minister. Someone important.

It wasn't until she came to the end of the lane and found herself actually confronted by it that she realized it was West Hill Court. It didn't look quite as huge as it had from a distance, but still it was huge enough. It had no less than eight windows on the second floor, plus three on either side of the front door and four more right up at the top, jutting out from under the roof. A green trelliswork veranda thing, covered in pink and purple climbing flowers, ran all the way around, forming a covered walkway, and a red-brick path with bits of moss and grass growing between the bricks led up to the door.

Bonny stopped, suddenly uncertain. She had known, of course, that Richard lived somewhere a bit grander than Factory Lane, but she hadn't imagined it would be anywhere quite as elegant as this. This was more sumptuous than anything she had ever seen.

As she stood there biting at a fingernail a car came scrunching up the gravel path and drew to a halt beside her. Bonny instinctively braced herself for trouble:

Who are you? What do you want? Don't you realize this is private property?

The car window was rolled down; a head poked out.

"Can I help you?"

It was a woman; thin and rather worried-looking. She had the same fair hair as Richard, and the same light, blue-green eyes. Bonny took her finger from her mouth.

"I'm looking for Richard."

"Richard?" The woman's face lit up. "Are you a friend of his?"

"Yes," said Bonny.

"From college?"

"Yes," said Bonny. "I mean—that is, not from his college. Another college. I came to see if he was here or if he's gone back yet."

"I'm afraid he has, he went back last week. But look, why don't you come in and—sorry! I should have introduced myself. I'm his mother. You're . . . ?"

"Bonny McEvoy."

"Bonny! Why don't you come in, Bonny, and have a cup of tea? Have you come very far?"

"From Crewe," said Bonny.

"Oh! That is a long way. In that case you must definitely come in—if you have the time, that is."

"All right," said Bonny. After all, it was still quite early, and it would be interesting to go inside and see what sort of place it was. She bet Jake had never been invited into anywhere so elegant.

She walked up the brick path to the front door while Mrs. Islip parked the car. She wished now that she hadn't said that bit about being at college. It had been stupid. What was going to happen if ever she came here with Richard and his mother said something about it? Richard would know that she was a liar. She would just have to pretend that it was a misunderstanding.

Mrs. Islip came up and opened the front door. Inside was a large square hallway, with a dark wooden floor covered in rugs and a staircase of the same sort of wood going up the middle.

"Come through," said Mrs. Islip. She led Bonny past the stairs and into a room that was all light and airy and smelling of flowers, with full-length windows looking out on to gardens. "Make yourself comfortable, Bonny, while I go and organize some tea. I shan't be a minute."

Bonny revolved slowly in the center of the room, taking it all in. This was the house she had told Jake about: the one that Nobby and Bo were buying. And she was going to live here, and have a pony, and learn to ride. She really *could* have a pony, if she lived in this house. The grounds stretched on forever, full of trees and flower beds and velvety grass, with what looked like wooded fields at the far end. Imagine if one day Richard were to inherit it, which he probably *would,* being the only boy, and they were to live here together and he would buy her a pony and teach her how to ride, and they would have two red setters and an old English sheepdog, and lots of free-range chickens all walking about the garden laying their eggs under the bushes, and they wouldn't ever eat any of them—the chickens, that is; they would eat the eggs, of course—and maybe they would have a cow as well, for milk, and a couple of goats, and they would all live here together and be happy and—

139

"There we are." Mrs. Islip had come back with a big silver tray full of tea things. "Take a seat, Bonny. How do you like your tea? Milk and sugar? Have a piece of gingerbread, it's one of Mrs. Alexander's specials. Richard loves Mrs. A.'s gingerbread. She always had to have a batch ready for him when he came back from school."

"What, every day?" said Bonny.

"At the end of term. When he came home for the holidays."

"You mean he had to go away?"

"To school."

Bonny wrinkled her nose. "Couldn't he have gone to school here?"

"Well . . . yes. I suppose he could. If we'd wanted. But his father . . ." Mrs. Islip trailed off. "It was his father's old school."

"I wouldn't want to go away," said Bonny, "if I lived somewhere like this."

"Kate doesn't go away. But it's different for boys. At least, I suppose—have another piece of gingerbread." She pushed the plate toward Bonny. "Where did you meet Richard? At college, did you say?"

"No." She was scotching that idea very firmly. "In London."

"Oh! Have you been with him in London?" Mrs. Islip leaned forward eagerly. "He's told me so little about it . . . He hasn't actually been home, you see. I just had these letters. First he wrote to say that he'd got himself a job; then a few days ago he wrote to say he was going back to Bristol."

So *that* was where he was at college. Bonny's heart lifted. She might not ever have been able to draw the

140

map of Great Britain to the geography teacher's satisfaction, but even she knew that Bristol wasn't a million
miles from Cheltenham.

Mrs. Islip scanned her face anxiously. "Did you
work with him, or—"

"Yes," said Bonny. "We did this telephoning job,
asking people what TV commercials they'd been
watching."

"*Richard?* Telephoned people?"

"Yes. It was great. You could go in just whenever
you wanted and leave when you wanted and go for tea
and coffee . . . It was all students. Students and people from the theater."

"And that's where you met?"

"Yes. Well, sort of. Like, when we were looking for
things—rooms, and things."

Mrs. Islip pounced. "Ah! That's what I've been
wanting to know: where did he live while he was in
London?"

"We had this place," said Bonny.

"You mean, you—you lived together?"

"Yes. Well—no. Not *together.*" Mrs. Islip wouldn't
like it if Bonny said that she and Richard had lived
together, sleeping in the same room. She would never
believe that they hadn't slept in the same bed. "We just
had digs in this same house."

"Ah." Mrs. Islip nodded. She didn't strike Bonny as
being as relieved as she might have been. She almost
gave the impression that she wouldn't have *minded* if
Richard and Bonny had lived together. Encouraged,
Bonny said, "Of course, we got to be quite friendly."

Mrs. Islip set down her tea cup.

"Did you? Did you really?"

141

"Yes. Well, I mean, being in the same house and all. You do, don't you?"

"It's just that Richard's never been one to make friends easily. I've been so worried about him, you can't imagine. If I'd known that he was with you—"

"Thing is," said Bonny, "I had to leave before he did. I had—"

"He should have brought you back with him for the weekend! Before going back to Bristol. We'd have been so pleased to see you. But he just went straight from London. I don't know—"

"This is it," said Bonny. "This is what I came to find out."

"What's that?"

"His address. At college. He was going to give it me, but we forgot."

"And yet he gave you his home address? Here in Cheltenham?"

"Yes," said Bonny. "He said, if ever I was down here—"

"That you should come by? Oh, I'm glad he did that! I'm really glad! That makes me very happy."

It made Bonny very happy too. She could almost believe that Richard *had* asked her to come by.

"Tell me," said Mrs. Islip. She spoke earnestly and confidentially. "Did he ever . . . talk to you at all?"

Bonny concentrated. "About what?"

"About—well! About himself."

She said guardedly, "He did a little bit."

"What sort of things did he talk about?"

"He talked about being at college. Doing medieval hist'ry."

"Nothing—personal?"

142

Bonny paused, considering what to say.

"Please don't think I'm asking you to give away any secrets," said Mrs. Islip.

Bonny didn't have any to give away. Richard never had told her anything personal. Not really personal. Not like she'd told him.

"I expect I'm just being a silly old fusspot of a mother. You know how it is." Mrs. Islip laughed. It sounded to Bonny rather a nervous sort of laugh. Richard's mother seemed to be rather a nervous sort of person. But quite nice. "You students! One can't help worrying over you; all mixed up and full of problems. Never seem to know where you're going or what you're doing. Drift out of one phase into another— because they *are* just phases. It's ridiculous to think that the way you are at eighteen is the way you're going to be for the rest of your life. I know I'm not the same now as I was when I was eighteen! I don't expect you're the same as you were when you were twelve. Are you?"

"No," said Bonny. She wondered what Mrs. Islip was talking about.

"It's what I've said all along: you grow out of things. I'm afraid Richard's father isn't quite as . . . well. It bothers him, you see. Anything to do with the children, it upsets him when they do things that, let's face it, lots of young people do nowadays. It's not like it was when we were young. Young people these days like to experiment. They like to try things out, like—well, like living together and—and all that kind of thing."

She paused hopefully. She seemed to be waiting for Bonny to say something.

"Gingerbread's good," said Bonny.

"I'm so glad you like it! It's always been one of Richard's favorites. Why don't you have some more?" Bonny helped herself to another slice.

"Nice grounds," she said.

"It is quite nice, isn't it? Do you like the land?"

"Yes," said Bonny. "My aunts live in a house that's got a thousand acres."

Mrs. Islip looked startled. "A thousand *acres*?"

"Well, or something like that. P'raps it's not quite a thousand. But it must be nearly. It goes on for miles. It's got donkeys, and a goat, and—" Bonny stopped, aghast. What was she *doing*? Jake was right: she told lies for no reason at all.

"You mean it's a sort of small farm?" said Mrs. Islip.

"Yes," said Bonny. "Have you got any donkeys?"

"No, I'm afraid we haven't. Kate's always on about getting some, but her father—well, it's not really practical. She's got her pony, of course. Do you ride, Bonny?"

Just in time, Bonny managed to prevent herself from saying yes. "Only donkeys. These donkeys that my aunts have in their house in the country—they used to live in Southampton, then they moved. That's why I had to leave London before I could get Richard's address. So if you could just let me have it . . ." If she could just let her have it, then Bonny could be on her way. It was all very pleasant, sitting here making conversation with Richard's mother and eating gingerbread, but what she really wanted to do was to go and find Richard. "If I could just make a note of it . . ."

"Yes. Well, I suppose . . ."

"He said," said Bonny. "He said I was to go and visit him. At college."

"Did he?" Mrs. Islip brightened. "Oh, well! If he said." Suddenly she seemed all happy and excited. "Let me go and get it for you. I have it out here somewhere, by the telephone . . . here we are! Twenty-nine Blenheim Crescent."

"Blennim?" said Bonny.

"Blenheim Crescent. Shall I write it down for you?"

After the address had been written down and Bonny had eaten yet another piece of gingerbread, Mrs. Islip said that she would give her a lift back to the station, to save her the long walk down the hill. They were just getting into the car when a girl wearing a green school uniform turned into the drive.

"Kate?" There was a sharp edge to Mrs. Islip's voice. "What are you doing home at this hour?"

"We had the last two periods off."

"Again? Are you sure?"

"Of course I'm sure!" The girl looked at her mother impatiently. "I wouldn't be here if I weren't, would I?"

Bonny thought, She's lying. She could spot a fellow liar when she saw one. She wouldn't have thought, though, that Richard's sister would be the sort to skip classes just whenever she felt like it.

"I don't want trouble," said Mrs. Islip, "like we had last time. If your father ever got to hear—"

"Oh, Ma, for heaven's sake! Stop going on."

"I'm not going on. But if your father—"

"If Pa gets to hear of it he'll burst a blood vessel. So who cares?" The girl glanced inquiringly toward Bonny. "Hello."

"This is Bonny," said Mrs. Islip. "She's a friend of Richard's. Bonny, this is Kate, my younger daughter."

The two girls studied each other. Kate wasn't a bit

like Richard. She had dark hair, thick and shoulder-length, and a round, rosy face with very brilliant brown eyes.

"Bonny met Richard in London," said Mrs. Islip. "They lived in the same house together. Now she's going down to Bristol to see him."

Kate didn't say anything to this, just went on looking at Bonny in speculative fashion, as if trying to decide which planet she came from. Her gaze wasn't hostile so much as curious, as if there were questions she would have liked to ask but couldn't with her mother around.

"I'm just giving Bonny a lift to the station," said Mrs. Islip.

"Okay. I'll probably be gone by the time you get back, I'm going down to the stables."

Mrs. Islip frowned and seemed on the point of saying something. As if to forestall her, Kate turned back abruptly to Bonny.

"When you see Richard, will you give him a message? Will you tell him that Kate said screw the lot of them?"

Her mother protested. "Kate! You can't ask Bonny to deliver a message like that."

"I can," said Kate. "I just have." She looked hard at Bonny. "You will give it him, won't you?"

"All right," said Bonny.

"It's very important. I want him to know that we're not *all* mealymouthed and small-minded."

"Kate," said Mrs. Islip. "Please don't."

"Why shouldn't I?" said Kate. She threw her hair back aggressively over her shoulders. "I think it's dis-*graceful,* the way he's been treated. Anyone would

146

think we were living in the Dark Ages—which of course we *are*, in this house."

Kate stalked off around the side beneath the trellis-work. Mrs. Islip and Bonny got into the car.

"You mustn't mind Kate," said Mrs. Islip. "She's just at that age."

Bonny sat, trying to puzzle things out. What did Mrs. Islip mean, just at that age? What age? Kate was the same age as herself; Richard had told her so. And what did Kate mean, saying it was disgraceful the way he had been treated? She would have liked to ask, except that it didn't seem quite polite, especially as Mrs. Islip was now talking about something quite different. Something about how she would willingly have driven Bonny all the way to Bristol if it weren't for having other things to do that afternoon, and did Bonny have enough money to get her there "because I know how you students are always broke."

"I expect I'll hitch a lift," said Bonny.

"Oh, no! No! You mustn't do that. You must promise me. I should never have a moment's peace. I'd sooner give you the train fare and know that you were safe. I insist," said Mrs. Islip.

She pulled the car up outside the station, took a wallet from her handbag, peeled off some notes, and pressed them into Bonny's hand, closing Bonny's fingers over them. She spoke breathlessly and all in a rush, almost as if she were embarrassed. "Tell Richard when you see him . . . tell him—tell him we love him very dearly, in spite of—of everything." She squeezed Bonny's hand. "Perhaps he'll bring you to visit us properly one of these days. I'd like that. But tell him, won't you, what I said?"

147

"Yes," said Bonny. And then, somewhat belatedly remembering her manners, "Thank you ever so much for the train fare," she added.

"My pleasure."

As the car pulled out of the station Bonny looked down at the notes in her hand. It seemed stupid to waste all that money on train fare when she could just as easily hitch a lift. After all, it was broad daylight, and Bristol couldn't be that far away.

On the other hand, how would Mrs. Islip feel if Bonny were discovered done to death in a highway ditch? She wouldn't be very happy. She would feel that Bonny had cheated her, taking her money and not using it. Or at any rate, not using it for the right purposes.

She sighed, stuffed the notes into the back pocket of her jeans, and turned into the station. Jake would say that she was an idiot; but she had the feeling that Richard would approve.

13
Chapter

Blenheim Crescent was a lot easier to get to than West Hill Court had been. It was only five minutes away from the station; an ordinary, suburban sort of street full of rather dreary-looking houses, tall and attached and a bit run-down. Number 29 had an old iron gate, sagging from a lopsided gatepost, and a scrubby patch of front yard with a yew tree, which dropped needles and had a bald area beneath it. Around the bald area sprouted dandelions and green weedy things and little clumps of grass. Bonny felt more at home in Blenheim Crescent than she had in West Hill Court.

At the side of the front door there were four bells, with little slots for names. The first slot had only half a name, because the other half had been ripped off; the half that was there said KEM. The second slot was empty; the third slot was illegible, because the ink had faded; and the fourth slot said HOUSEKEEPER, with a handwritten note taped beneath it announcing in uncertain capital letters that THE HOOSIEKEEPERIS AT NO 40. After studying it awhile, Bonny came to the conclusion that the housekeeper must be foreign.

She wondered which of the remaining three bells to try first. KEM obviously wasn't Richard, and upon closer inspection the one that had faded almost to nothing looked as if it said Snood, or maybe Snode, but at any rate not Islip. That left only number 2. She pressed it.

After a second or so there came the sound of a sash window being rattled open, and a voice from above called out, "Hello?" Bonny took a step backward and looked up. A woman was leaning out.

"Who did you want?"

"I'm looking for Richard Islip."

"Top apartment, but I'm not sure that they're in. One of them might be. Hang on, I'll go and yell up the stairs."

It had never occurred to Bonny that Richard might be sharing. It ought to since almost everybody did, but somehow she had always pictured him as being on his own. She hoped his roommate wasn't someone horrid.

A ghastly and appalling thought suddenly came to her: suppose it was a *girl*?

The woman came back and leaned out of the window again.

"Jan's there. He's coming down."

Yan? What kind of a name was Yan? Perhaps she meant Ian.

150

Well, whatever she meant, at least it wasn't a girl; that was the main thing.

"Thank you very much," said Bonny.

"You're welcome."

The woman withdrew, pushing the window closed behind her. A moment later the front door was flung open. A boy stood there. He was smallish and dark, with wiry black hair and very bright blue eyes, wearing jeans and a red sweatshirt that said NIBBLES & BYTES in bold white letters across the front.

"Hello!" He sounded quite friendly.

"Hello," said Bonny.

"Did you want Richard? He's not back yet. D'you want to come up and wait? He shouldn't be too long, he's usually in around about now. Come up and have a coffee or something."

Bonny followed him up the stairs, which he took three and four at a time, leaping catlike in his Nikes.

"Are you Bonny?" he said. "Richard's told me about you. I hear you've been organizing him."

"Dunno about organizing," said Bonny.

"Well, bullying." The boy turned, as they reached the top landing, and grinned. "He needs bullying. Left to himself he just waffles. Come on in!"

He ushered her before him into a large, extremely untidy room with a sloping ceiling.

"Take a seat—if you can find one. Chuck some of that junk off the sofa. Shove it on the floor. I'll go and make some coffee." He went through into what Bonny could see was a tiny kitchen, almost no bigger than a cupboard. "I'm Jan, by the way."

Bonny moved a large bundle of computer printouts

to the far end of the sofa and squeezed herself into a small space between two piles of clothes.

"What sort of a name is Jan?" she said.

"Polish. Like the pianist." Jan stuck his head back around the door. "I'm Kempinski, he was Paderewski. How d'you like your coffee? Weak, strong, or just as it comes?"

"Anyhow'll do. What's 'Nibbles and Bytes' mean?"

"Computer terms."

"It sounds like a pop group."

"I thought of starting a pop group once. Atomic Waste, I was going to call it. Then Rickie came along and I got sort of sidetracked. Not into pop music, our Rick."

"Is that what you call him?" said Bonny.

"Only when I'm feeling happy with him. Why? What do you call him?"

"Just Richard."

Mostly, Richard had said, that was what everybody called him. Bonny swiveled around on the sofa, taking in the details of the room. It was full of clutter. It had to be Jan's; Richard didn't like clutter. He had always been the one to do the tidying up, to clear the fireplace of empty cans and take out the rubbish.

Behind her a second door was open. Bonny craned forward: a bedroom. She could just see one end of an unmade bed and a bedside table containing two empty beer bottles and a heap of books. Cautiously, because it did seem a bit like spying, she left the sofa and tiptoed across. In one corner stood an old-fashioned wardrobe, dark and heavy, with suitcases piled high on the top; in the other corner a second bed, neatly made as if it had never been slept in.

152

Bonny wondered which of the beds was Richard's, or whether perhaps there was another bedroom elsewhere in the apartment. It didn't somehow seem very likely. Still, she wouldn't object to sleeping on the sofa for a bit, just until she and Richard could find somewhere else. Or maybe Jan would find somewhere else. Or maybe they could all live together as a threesome. She would keep the place clean for them, and do the shopping and learn how to cook, and in return Richard would give her lessons so that one day she could take exams and go to college, and up yours, Jake Armitage. Just because *he* hadn't been clever enough—

"Coffee!"

Bonny sprang around guiltily. "I was just looking at the apartment."

"Apartment, she calls it! Glorified studio. Mind you, I gather in London he really had to pig it: no hot water, no heated towel rails, no separate shower unit." Jan chuckled happily. "Must have been quite an eye-opener!"

"It wasn't as bad as all that," said Bonny. "It wasn't a *slum*. Of course, it wasn't quite the same as Cheltenham."

"I'll bet it wasn't! You ever been to Cheltenham?"

"Yes." She said it proudly. "I met Richard's mother. Have you met Richard's mother?"

"Yeah, I've met her."

"She's nice, isn't she?"

"Very nice."

"She said I was to go and see her again, with Richard."

"Did she?" Jan regarded her thoughtfully a moment over the rim of his coffee mug. His eyes were bluer

153

than anybody's eyes, almost, that she had ever seen. "Tell me, did you—" He broke off, as from somewhere outside came the sound of a whistle. "Hang about!" He set the mug down. "That'll be Rickie now. I'll go and tell him you're here."

He bounded out through the door. He was like a rubber ball, thought Bonny; all leaping and bouncing. She wondered why Richard had never mentioned him. She had never mentioned Jake, of course, but that was different. She had mentioned Donovan and Julie.

"There you go!" Jan had reappeared with Richard a few paces behind him. He waved a hand. "All yours."

Bonny felt suddenly bashful, seeing Richard again. It seemed that he felt the same way, for he stood awkwardly in the doorway, a briefcase in one hand, a pile of books under his arm, as stiff and embarrassed as the day when they had first met. It was left to Jan to break the silence.

"Well, I'll leave you to it. I'm going out for a while. I've got some stuff to look up in the library." He held out a hand to Bonny. "Cheers!"

"What about your coffee?" said Richard.

"You can have it."

The door closed. They heard Jan's footsteps receding down the stairs. They stood, looking at each other.

"I'm sorry about going off like I did," said Bonny.

"Going off? Oh! You mean, back to Crewe. That's okay." Richard tossed his briefcase and books onto an already overcrowded armchair. "I understood. You wanted to be with Jake."

Bonny's head jerked up. "How did you—"

"Elaine told me."

That *cow*. "Did you see her, after I'd gone?"

154

"Only at work." He perched himself on the arm of the chair, cradling Jan's discarded coffee mug. "Did the old ladies write to you?"

"What old ladies?"

"Nobby and Bo."

"Nobby and *Bo*?"

"I looked in on them. On my way back. I thought, while I had a bit of time to kill, I'd just go and check the place out. Just to—"

To what? Satisfy curiosity?

Something more complex. In an odd sort of way he had felt drawn to go back there; had felt compelled to gaze once again upon the spot where he and Bonny had stood that first night, hammering on the door. *Is there anybody there?*

He had half expected the cottage to have disappeared, to have been bulldozed out of existence and the foundations already laid for a three-story apartment house. He had been surprised to find it not only still intact but all spruced up with a fresh coat of paint and quite obviously inhabited. What impulse it was that had led him to go up the tiny front path and rat-tat with the brass horseshoe knocker he was not quite sure even now. He had certainly not anticipated the old ladies being there.

"Apparently, what happened, the place was riddled with dry rot. They had to have it practically rebuilt, so they simply took the cats and decamped for a few weeks."

Bonny was staring at him, big-eyed. "You talked to them?"

He had done more than talk to them, he had actually stayed the night. They had insisted. To begin with,

155

it was they who had done all the talking: Nobby, short and dumpy, with little dimpled hands; Bo tall and imperious, rather headmistressy. They had talked mainly about Bonny, telling him of the difficulties she had had as a child, telling him how greatly she had improved, the efforts she had made.

"We've often thought, if she could only have come to us earlier . . . But fourteen, you see. It's just that little bit too late."

"And the school hardly helped, saying she was ineducable."

"Bonny's not ineducable!" Richard had been quite indignant. "That's a criminal thing to say!"

They had warmed to him for that. They had agreed, hotly, that it *was* criminal.

"I'm sure all she needs is the right kind of guidance—"

"The right kind of en*courage*ment."

"Someone who would teach her to respect herself."

"To put a *value* on herself."

"A boyfriend," said Nobby, "who would help pull her *up* instead of dragging her down."

They had looked hopefully at Richard as they spoke. He had known what they would have liked him to say; he had felt he was letting them down by not saying it. But they had seemed to understand. After a bit, after they had pressed him to stay the night, they had started asking him about himself. They were sympathetic—Nobby especially, though Bo perhaps was the more perceptive of the two. They had drawn him out, got him talking in a way no one else ever had. He had told them about Jan.

"Did they . . . ask after me?" said Bonny.

"Of course they did! What do you think? They hadn't heard from you since Christmas; they were getting quite worried. They said they'd sent you a postcard just recently, telling you about the cottage. They couldn't understand why you hadn't been in touch."

"Did you tell them?" said Bonny. "Did you tell them it was because I wasn't there?"

"Yes, I told them."

"What did they say?"

"They said they were going to write to you again."

"When? Soon?"

"Well, yes, I suppose. I don't really know. They probably thought if you'd gone back to Crewe you'd have gotten their postcard."

"No!" That was Donovan and Julie, that was, not telling her. The card must have come while she was in London.

"I'd thought perhaps," said Richard, "that you were on your way down there."

"How could I be? I thought they weren't *there*—I thought they'd *moved*!"

A silence fell. Richard didn't ask the obvious question. If Bonny were not on her way to Southampton to see the old ladies, then . . . He wasn't sure that he wanted to know the answer. He had grown fond of Bonny during the time they had spent together. He had thought of her often these past few weeks. He wouldn't like to have to say anything that would hurt or distress her.

Abruptly, he tipped the remains of Jan's coffee down his throat. "Have you eaten?"

"Not since earlier."

"What's earlier?"

157

" 'Bout three o'clock. I had gingerbread cake," said Bonny, "with your mother."

"My *mother*?"

"Yes." She gave him the old, defiant tilt of the chin. "I went to see her. I had to. I didn't have your address at the university."

"But—" How had she found his address in Cheltenham? He might just conceivably have given her 29 Blenheim Crescent; he would never in a million years have given her West Hill Court.

"I looked it up," said Bonny, "didn't I? In the telephone directory."

"And then you went to see her?"

"Well, you went to see Nobby and Bo."

The implication was clear enough: if he had gone to see Nobby and Bo, why shouldn't Bonny go to see his mother? He wondered uncomfortably what kind of things they had talked about.

"Actually, I am quite hungry," said Bonny.

"Okay." He stood up. "Let's go down the road and get something."

He took her to the Pizza di Roma, which he and Jan sometimes went to because it was out of the way and not jam-packed with students. It was the sort of place where you could be private and talk.

"I couldn't stand Crewe anymore," said Bonny. "Not after London."

He frowned. "What about Jake?"

"Couldn't stand him anymore, either," said Bonny. She twirled some loops of spaghetti around her fork. "Not after being with you."

Richard said nothing, but felt the palms of his hands grow moist. He was going to have to tell her.

158

"He kept on," said Bonny, "about me being stupid."

"You're not stupid."

"I wrote off like you said, to the open university, and he said they wouldn't let me in there. He said I was too stupid."

"I told you," said Richard, "they'll let anyone in there. And you're not stupid."

There was a pause. Bonny went on twirling. "Anyway," she said, "they'll have the wrong address now 'cause I've left."

"You'll have to write and tell them."

"I will," said Bonny. "Just as soon as I know where I'm going to be."

Richard bit his lip. "What did my mother have to say? Anything interesting?"

"She gave me a message for you. She said to tell you . . ." Bonny concentrated, trying to get it right. "That in spite of everything they still loved you. That was what she said. And your sister said to tell you, screw the lot of them."

He smiled very faintly. Trust Kate . . .

"What did she mean?" said Bonny.

"She meant—" How could he explain what Kate had meant? "She meant what you were always telling me: stand up for yourself."

"Oh." Bonny chewed solemnly at a mouthful of spaghetti. She seemed to be pondering. "What did your mother mean, *in spite of everything*?"

He shook his head.

"She said you hadn't been home," said Bonny. "She said you'd gone straight from London back to Bristol."

"Yes."

"Did you have a row or something?"

159

"Not exactly a row."

"Something that you did?"

"Something . . . personal."

Bonny sat waiting. "You don't have to tell me if you don't want to," she said.

"It's all right. It's not a secret." Not anymore. Be true to yourself, that was what the old ladies had said. "I don't mind telling you, but you—you mightn't like it."

"Why mightn't I like it?"

"You mightn't like *me*."

"I will like you!" Whatever he'd done, it couldn't be anything terrible. Not really terrible. And even if it were, she would still like him. "Try me," she said.

What have you got to be ashamed of? That was what Bo had asked him. Deep down, inside yourself . . . *ARE* you ashamed?

Deep down inside himself he wasn't. But on the surface, at the level where it counted, with other people—

"*Try* me!" said Bonny.

"It's nothing very dramatic. I haven't murdered anyone or anything. It's just that—" He pushed his hair back off his forehead. "At the end of last term, I—I took Jan back home with me for a couple of days."

Bonny looked at him.

"I told them," said Richard, "that we were . . . living together."

"So?"

"So they hadn't realized. It came as a—shock."

A frown wrinkled Bonny's brow. She plainly wasn't with him. In Jan's voice, he thought, You'll have to do better than this, my son.

"When I say living together, I mean—living to-

160

gether. Like—" He swallowed. "Like . . . *being* together. Like a couple."

The penny dropped. Bonny's face grew slowly crimson.

"He's a pouf," Jake said.

"He's not!" she'd told him.

"Course he is," said Jake.

All right. So he was. So *what*? Bonny twirled vigorously with her fork in her spaghetti. "What'd you have
to go and tell them for? 'S asking for trouble. Might
have known they wouldn't like it."

"Well . . ." He shrugged a shoulder. He felt
strangely calm now that he had broken it to Bonny.
Strangely at peace. "It just seemed right that they
should know."

"Why?" said Bonny.

"Because one can't keep on living a lie, I suppose."

She fell silent at that.

"Bonny?" Richard stretched out a hand across the
table. "I'm sorry."

"No need to be sorry. Nothing to be sorry about.
Not your fault."

"I feel I should have told you before."

"Don't see why. Can't be expected to go around
wearing a badge, can you?"

"Well—no." Not even Jan had expected that of him.
"I didn't mean that. I—"

"Got nice eyes," said Bonny, "hasn't he? Nice and
blue." She munched on her spaghetti. "I s'pose he's
quite good-looking, really."

"Yes, I—I suppose he is."

"Are you in love with him?"

161

Richard felt the prickles break out down his spine. Even the Pizza di Roma wasn't as private as all that.

"No reason why you shouldn't be," said Bonny. "No law against it, is there?"

No, there wasn't any law against it.

"So what's the problem?"

The problem at that moment was Bonny herself.

"Bonny," he said, "I—"

Bonny pushed her plate away. "I ought to be going now. 'S getting late."

"Where are you going to go?"

"Go back to Southampton. 'Bout time I saw Nobby and Bo. They'll be wondering what's happened to me."

"You don't have to rush off. You're very welcome to stay the night if you'd like to."

"No. I ought to get back." Determinedly she hauled her canvas bag onto the table. If she were going to go, then she wanted to go immediately. "I only just dropped by to give you this."

He took the book that she was holding out to him. *Down and Out?* It was a bit more tattered than when he had originally lent it to her. Some of the pages were dog-eared, and there was a coffee ring on the front cover. "Why don't you keep it?" he said. "I can always get another."

"All right," said Bonny. "I'll keep this one, and you can have this." From the depths of the bag she produced her copy of *Forever Amber.* "You ought to read that, if you're doing medieval hist'ry."

Gravely, he said that he would. "I'll write and let you know how I get on with it."

"Will you?" said Bonny.

"Or maybe we'll come down. Nobby and Bo—"

162

They had made him promise, while he was there: "Bring your young man down to see us sometime." Jan had laughed when he heard the description.

"Young man already!"

"That's only because they don't know you," Richard had said crushingly.

"We could always drive down one weekend," he said. "I mean, if you'd like us to?"

"Shouldn't think it's a question of whether I'd like you to," said Bonny, "as whether you've still got transport." She stood up, slinging the canvas bag over her shoulder. "That heap of junk they palmed you off with . . . I'm surprised it's still going."

He didn't tell her that it was temporarily off the road. He had already had a mouthful from Jan on the subject of poor little rich boys who allowed themselves to be conned; he could do without a repeat dose from Bonny.

He walked back with her to the station and sent her off to call the old ladies while he bought her ticket. Fortunately there was a train due in at any minute.

"Glad we haven't got to wait," said Bonny. "Can't stand waiting."

"You will be all right by yourself, won't you?"

"Course I will! I'm always all right by myself. I'd have been all right by myself that first day when I met you."

"Would you rather you hadn't met me?"

"Don't s'pose so."

"I certainly wouldn't rather I hadn't met *you*. Jan says . . ." He hesitated, wondering if he were being diplomatic. "Jan says when I went away I was a hundred percent useless."

Bonny's lip quivered. "Don't see what he sees in you if that's what he thinks."

"Well, but he doesn't think it now—thanks to you."

"Don't know what I'm s'posed to have done."

"You made me live like a squatter, for a start! You made me eat canned tomatoes and condensed milk and steal things from supermarkets."

"G-*gosh!*" said Bonny.

He grinned. "Are you teasing me?"

"Might be. Might not be." She wiped the back of her hand across her nose. "This my train?"

"Looks like it." On impulse he bent and kissed her. "Give my love to Nobby and Bo. Tell them we'll be down very soon."

As the train drew away, Bonny leaned out of the window and called after him, "Don't forget to read that book I gave you. You ought to read it if you're doing medieval hist'ry."

He supposed after that he would have to.

About the Author

Jean Ure is the author of many novels, including *You Win Some, You Lose Some* and *After Thursday,* both available in Delacorte Press editions. She lives in England.